ELISABETH RYNELL

# TO MERVAS

Translated from the Swedish by Victoria Häggblom

*archipelago books*

Library of Congress Cataloging-in-Publication Data
Rynell, Elisabeth, 1954–
[Till Mervas. English]
To Mervas : a novel / by Elisabeth Rynell ; translated from the Swedish by Victoria Häggblom.
p. cm.
ISBN 978-0-9819873-7-8
I. Häggblom, Victoria. II. Title.
PT9876.28.Y6T5513 2010
823'.92--dc22      2008016760

Archipelago Books
232 Third Street, #A111
Brooklyn, NY 11215
www.archipelagobooks.org

Distributed in the U.S.A. and Canada by Consortium Books Sales and Distribution
www.cbsd.com

Distributed in the U.K. and Europe by Turnaround Publisher Services
www.turnaround-uk.com

This publication was made possible by the generous support of Lannan Foundation, the
Barbro Osher Pro Suecia Foundation, the Swedish Arts Council, the National Endowment for the Arts, and the New York State Council on the Arts, a state agency.

NATIONAL
ENDOWMENT
FOR THE ARTS

NYSCA

Manufactured at Thomson-Shore, Inc. in Dexter, Michigan
Visit Thomson-Shore on the web at www.thomsonshore.com

Life must be a story,
or else it will crush you.

I've been thinking that just like a fire,
a story too has its place, its hearth.

From there it rises and burns.
Devours its tale.

# TO MERVAS

I

A letter came. Just a few lines, jotted down on a piece of copy paper.

> *Marta, Mart! I'm in Mervas. It's not possible to get*
> *any farther away. And no closer either. Your Kosti.*

That's all it said. And he hadn't been in touch for over twenty years. Not that I've been counting the years; I stopped doing that a long time ago. But now he'd sent me this message and it was like being filled with air, like being hit in the face by a gale so strong it made me gasp for breath.

I read the letter again and again. My first thought was that it was fake, that someone wanted to taunt me. But who would want to do that? I have no friends; there's no one who would know that such a cryptic little note would weigh on me. No one, except perhaps Kosti himself. And now he had written it. A faint cry from one end of life to the other, a cry straight through the years. And from Mervas. What kind of place was Mervas?

I wept. A sadness so vast washed over me I wasn't sure I'd be able to contain it. In some ways, it was myself that I mourned. I mourned my own life; it was as if I'd been invited to my own funeral and now stood above

---

the coffin, where everything had been completed and settled, where for the first time my life could be looked upon as something finished and concluded, and there was nothing, absolutely nothing, that could be added to it. And I cried over everything that was lost, everything that had gone wrong and been led astray. My tears were unnaturally hot, they ran down my neck and onto my chest and I felt their entire path, felt how hot they were, strangely, remarkably hot, as if there'd been boiling, volcanic wells hidden inside me, and now they were overflowing through my eyes.

To keep from falling to pieces, I started pacing. I covered every room. The small, dismal apartment became a dreamscape. My tears made everything blurry, almost blotted things out, and in this intense and charged absence, I reached for objects like a blind person. I used my fingertips to see, my eyes were elsewhere.

I must have plodded for hours. The entire time, I thought I would implode from sadness, that I would break like a clay vessel in pressured heat. I touched potted plants, rocks, books, furniture, and lamp shades. It grew darker in the rooms, I could sense the gloam through my skin. The midday gray seeped inside and settled on the floor, the walls, and grew denser.

In my head echoed the idiotic little saying "A letter means so much." I couldn't get rid of it; the insinuating voice followed me wherever I went. I knew that the letter I'd received wasn't much of a letter, but still, the few words he'd written were alive inside me, they'd awakened and shaken me, struck me with something I'd nearly lost. They'd reminded me of my life and the fact that I was still living it, that I was supposed to live it. I'd forgotten that. I'd stayed away from that truth. And a person can actually hide inside her own life, hide from life itself within the minutiae and everyday chores, hide from herself inside herself. She can do it, I know this, I knew it even then, but I didn't pay it any mind.

———

Finally, I went to the bathroom and turned on the light. Avoiding my reflection in the mirror, I filled the sink with cold water and submerged my hot, tear-swollen face. I held it in the ice-cold water until it ached. Then I straightened slowly and met my image in the mirror. I have never liked my face; I've somehow never been able to pull it together. Here it was, large and unignorable, looming in the mirror like an approaching storm. It was an old face, I could see that. Ugly. The ugly face stared back at me and simultaneously, in an alarming maneuver, crawled inside me and stared out at itself. I was old and ugly and here I stood. A letter from the other end of time had arrived and the blind and complacent one-day-at-a-time existence I'd been living for so many years had instantly burst to pieces. Instead, I now held my entire life, my whole story, in my arms, and it looked like a skinned animal, a skinned yet still living, struggling animal. I shook from holding it, shook from the very core of my being. And as I stood there, the thought went through my mind that I'd waited for him my entire life. My whole adult life I'd longed for him, kept a small place ready, a little backyard, a secret, hidden place for him, for Kosti. I knew that this place had been the only one that mattered, the one thing that had kept me alive, even though I myself didn't even know it existed. Now I'd discovered it. I'd caught myself in the act. I too had been carried along by a dream. Simply being alive isn't enough. Perhaps that's how it must be.

I stood captive before the bathroom mirror and stared into the face that was supposed to be mine. Once you get lost in your life, I thought, you just keep getting more and more lost. Meanwhile, the years close in on you like a thick forest. They tangle and grow denser, they become tangled forests of years.

The apartment now lay in darkness. Mervas, I thought dimly. What kind of place is Mervas? I stood in the kitchen and the lamp over the kitchen table was lit. His letter lay there, exposed. Written in blue ink. I'd avoided letting my tears fall onto it. He'd always used blue ink that tears could dissolve. *Your Kosti*, it said. *Your Kosti*, he'd written. How could he? Only those who are truly alone know what it's like to be a lost child in the world, a lost child in a great war. But all of us are alone, more or less. Someone lost us along the way. With my hands still trembling slightly, I refolded the paper and put it back inside the envelope. No more tears were coming, no hot tears. The wells had evidently dried up. All I felt was a dry cramping in my chest, a feeling of something inconsolable draining me, feeding off me. I wasn't feeling sorry for myself, I think, not even then. I'm not worth pitying. But my life hurt inside me. It moved like a child, like a fetus inside me, a bundle of hammering, kicking willpower. This is unbearable, I remember thinking. Only that single word: unbearable.

Somewhere in my life is a city shrouded in darkness. It's a big city, probably a capital. All roads lead to it, into the dark, where they dissolve. I know this city exists, that like all cities it has houses and streets, that a kind of living takes place there, stories are formed, meetings and scenes. But nothing can be distinguished in that darkness. It is like a mute weave that has been pushed into the center of my life, thread upon thread of silence. And I'm afraid of this darkness, I know that from it, anything can break through: a bright, blind violence, a rage like a forest fire igniting even the air. There are monsters living there that have courted me, monsters that hatch in darkness, and I don't want to see them, don't want to know about them. Sometimes I imagine that the city gulps down the darkness, that it greedily fills itself with more and more darkness and grows, swells – and in this way, it is active, a volcano in reverse. A crater that drinks and devours rather than spewing things out.

Standing there by the kitchen table looking at the envelope where I'd just put Kosti's letter, I suddenly caught a glimpse of the dark city, as if it had been illuminated in a flash of light. A bright white sheen pumped through it like a heartbeat, and I realized I had to enter it, perhaps it wasn't always sunk in darkness; light could blow into it, a wind of light.

Now it was really evening, and I felt I had to get out, had to leave my apartment, get away from everything that had settled in its walls, the sour breathing of years that felt as if it would suffocate me. I took a comb from the bathroom cabinet and pulled it lovelessly through my shoulder-length, nowadays thin gray hair. After that, I painted my lips red and dabbed some powder on my large-pored skin, swollen from crying. Have to get out of the apartment, I thought, perhaps down to the store to buy some food, anything.

It was after suppertime. November. The air had gotten cold and spots on the ground that used to be wet had turned into ice. There was a faint wind and I walked around the block. Three-story buildings were arranged around the yards like loaves of bread, and there were a few single-family houses on display. These were residential neighborhoods, the streets seemed bored; the whole area caught in a suppressed yawn. I walked on listlessly, and suddenly stood outside the front door of my building again. I had nowhere to go and the mere thought of the grocery store made me anxious, it was too bright in there for me tonight, I didn't want to walk around with a basket on my arm and have to pick and choose; it seemed impossible, disgusting. So without actually making any kind of decision, I walked over to a small neighborhood restaurant that had recently opened, a place I'd never been before and never even considered going, because I don't go to restaurants. I walked in and sat down at a table. I had the remarkable feeling that everything was an illusion, a liberating sensation of not being myself but someone else, perhaps someone in a movie, someone outside myself I could watch and perhaps pretend to be for a little while. I ordered food and a small carafe of red wine and a little later another glass of red wine and a pack of cigarettes. Except, it wasn't really me, it was the woman in the movie who did all this. She was a tired middle-aged woman, just like me, but far more interesting and confident. She was now getting a little drunk sitting in the small, cozy space, its red dimness reflecting her life back to her like a crystal ball. She saw all the images and allowed them to emerge without resisting. She sat there gazing into the beautiful red wine in her glass while the thoughts and images in her mind drifted freely: it was as if she saw her life inside that glass and she leaned over it in order to take a close, careful look.

A letter has come, I thought, and a sudden fearlessness filled me: I wanted somehow to feel how time had passed, all those years after Kosti, how my life turned out, how everything turned out. I dared thinking about the fact that I had been a mother: even someone like me had become a mother by giving birth to a child, a boy, my deformed boy, unfit for life. And now I saw the years, months, hours, and minutes bound to him, the peculiar slowness, millimeter upon millimeter of the gray, faintly buzzing slowness I'd felt together with him. It was like a period of timelessness injected into my life, and when I looked into the glass, I saw those years, saw them moving faintly down there on the bottom. I'd been absorbed by timelessness back then; I'd let myself be nourished by it. I'd been a mother during those years after Kosti, a mother to a helpless child, and even though this child was no longer alive, I dared to think I'd gone on being his mother, and that I'd kept living with him in that timelessness. Perhaps that's why I'd been hit so hard by Kosti's letter; he'd jolted me into the present. And that hurt. Timelessness is a kind of death that attracts those who cannot or do not have the courage to live. But despite my pain, I also noticed that something had awakened in me during the day and it was calling me, there was something intriguing about the memories and images that flashed through me as I drank. It was as if I'd been missing myself for a very long time. As if I'd been standing abandoned for a very long time.

The boy's face. Heavy and impossible to read. The mouth without control and constantly glistening wet, a mere cavity that had happened to end up in his face. He couldn't reach his own mouth, couldn't access it fully. It was as if a thread, the link that connected him to his own body, had been severed. His legs and hands were also half-asleep, somehow muddled. He couldn't reach himself anywhere.

Except his eyes. He existed through his eyes. His gaze reached out from that big, lifeless body, found its way past an otherwise meaninglessly constructed face. From the moment he was born, his gaze had been the same. And it seized me. From the very beginning, there was an intimacy between us so profound that as soon as I recognized it, I knew I'd never be able to escape it. His gaze went straight into my life.

I remember the first few days after his birth as a quake. A quake that reached all the way to the center of the earth. I had just delivered, felt so recently opened. At the same time, I burned with a sense of presence. They left me alone with him for twenty-four hours. Then they came and tore us apart. They stole my boy.

It was at the radiology ward, you know, where there are lots of odd little booths with drapes covering the open doors. I sat in one of those booths and waited for them to return with my boy. The booths around me were empty: the whole place seemed deserted. Perhaps it was the weekend. During the night, my breasts had filled with something that felt like cement. They were enormous. Rock hard. So tender that even the light feeling of my clothes against my skin made me shiver with pain. I thought I was the one who had just been born. I was as newly born as my small child that they'd just carried away. And in this strange new world, nothing existed but him, nothing but the child, only his gaze, his smell, and the feeling of his small, eager mouth searching for my nipples.

I remember that it took a while. Then I heard steps, and voices far away in the maze of booths. I sat, alert, and listened. A man's voice called out:

"I've found a space in ward nineteen!"

I'd already left the booth and ran like a blind person through the maze. Suddenly, I saw the doctor standing there, the one who'd called out, and I threw myself at him.

"Where's my boy?" I screamed, my fists hitting his chest. "Where have you taken my child?"

"Calm down!" the doctor yelled, and grabbed my wrists. "Calm down a little, and I'll explain."

But I wasn't calm. I tried to drag him in the direction where I thought they'd taken my boy.

"Give me back my child right now!" I screamed. "I want my child, I want my child, I want – "

I burst into tears, and the doctor I had attacked a moment earlier put his arm around me and led me into a booth.

"Try and pull yourself together. I'm going to explain what's going on," he said formally and rather sternly. He took a pencil from the breast pocket of his shirt, and I hated him. Go on, talk, I thought. I know you're lying. I know you've taken away my son to slaughter him. My hatred was so intense it ought to have made him dissolve like a fly in an acid bath.

"You're going to slaughter my son," I said.

"No, we're not. We're going to try to help him. Your son is gravely ill and I insist that you make an effort to listen to me."

He drew something on the paper that covered the examination table inside the booth and explained how something was very wrong inside the boy's head. I didn't believe what he was saying, and listened with only half an ear since I was sure they'd taken the boy to slaughter him. I knew I was the only thing my boy needed, and it was up to me to save him.

"I want to go to ward nineteen, where my child is," I said as soon as the doctor had finished talking.

"You can't do that," he said. "You have to go back to the maternity ward first. They have to discharge you there before you can come back to the children's ward."

"Then the police will have to come and take me back to the maternity ward. I'm going to my boy now."

I felt strong enough to upend the whole hospital, if necessary.

The doctor thought I was being difficult and couldn't hide his irritation. Finally, he gave in a little.

"You know, there's no room for you in ward nineteen anyway. It's an intensive care ward. You can't stay there overnight."

We then made our way in silence through the big hospital over to the remote children's ward where they'd taken my child.

Entering the dimly lit room where the boy was supposed to be, I thought for a moment I'd ended up in Hieronymus Bosch's Hell. Fetuses with tubes and hoses taped everywhere on their perplexing little bodies lay in their incubators, exposed in the strong lights like ancient relics or the crown jewels in a museum's glass case. Around the room, between these incubators, were transparent carts with infants, and I immediately focused on a baby with shiny white pieces of tape on its face. The tape seemed to hold the unnaturally round cheeks together. I was filled with violent disgust at the thought that they had to tape the child's cheeks to keep them in place, that otherwise they would fall away to each side like two loose lumps. My gaze searched the dim room and there, at the farthest end, I spotted the boy. The first thing I saw was that they'd taped his cheeks too. Narrow white strips appeared to tear his tiny face apart; it was as if they had marked him like a sacrificial animal.

At the sight of the boy, my breasts, which all day had been on the verge of exploding from the pressure of the hardening cement filling them, began to leak. I closed my eyes and leaned over the bed to finally inhale his scent, to feel his skin against mine. When I carefully folded the blanket aside to lift him up, I saw that the tape on his cheeks held a thin tube in place. It was placed inside one of his nostrils. A tube. A feeding tube. They don't want me to feed him anymore, I thought. He would no longer get to lie in my arms and catch my nipple to drink with his whimsical, eager mouth. The doctors thought this boy was so sick he didn't need a mother. He'd get a new, clinical mother; someone approved of, perhaps even a man.

I remember that I shook with a sense of injustice; it moved through every cell in my body. For a while, I stood and cried with the boy pressed against me. Then I put him back in the bed and went out to the nearby reception area. At a desk, a doctor was talking on the phone.

"Why have you given my child a feeding tube?" I asked, trying my utmost to remain calm, to not throw up, to not rush up to the man by the desk and start hitting him with the phone.

"Could you hold on a second?" he said. "As you can see, I'm on the phone."

"I want to know why you've given my child a feeding tube!" I screamed. "He can eat on his own. I'm going to feed him. Me! You hear me? He's my child!"

"Sorry," the doctor said into the phone. "I think I've got a nursing-crazed mother on my hands."

He turned to me. I saw the horns in his forehead.

"Which child are you referring to?" he asked.

The days that followed were like a slow descent into a warped underground realm, an abyss where faces in gaudy colors floated through the air, their voices snapping as if they had fangs. I searched for the boy everywhere, and everywhere he was taken away from me, following protocol after protocol according to regulations so sacred they couldn't be questioned by anyone in heaven or on earth.

"We think the feeding tube is more practical because then we'll know exactly how much he eats. We can send a breast pump to your room, so maybe eventually we'll let you bottle-feed him," someone said.

The first few days I tried to defend myself by transforming into a bear mother, a lioness, a tigress. But the high priests weren't scared by any mother animals, they didn't understand the meaning of words like mother, milk, mouths; they didn't understand what thousands of years of deep dark knowledge and desire can awaken in a human being. They didn't realize how close they were to driving me insane when they ignored the inner forces that threatened to tear me apart.

One evening when I sat in the little hospital room I had demanded, a nurse came to me and whispered:

"Don't sit here pumping. Bring the baby in here and nurse him. Screw the doctors, they don't understand anything."

But by then it was too late; the claws of the tigress had already been trimmed, her teeth pulled out. The milk was drying up, and I didn't dare try placing the child on my breast.

It would probably have been good for the boy to nurse. And for me too. When he was a week old, one of his arms began twitching strangely, and at the same time he started crying. And the crying never ceased. It went on day and night, every waking moment, and sometimes even when he slept. His cries were sometimes hoarse and exhausted, other times high and shrill.

But in the midst of this wailing, his gaze was alive, the boy's gaze. It pierced through his tears. And it was insistent. Insistent that the world give him an answer.

Mervas existed. Yes, it exists. I found it in the index of a big Nordic atlas in the library. Mervas, it read suddenly, and I almost started with surprise. I'd found it! I got the strange idea that no one before me had ever looked it up in this atlas. Mervas was listed just for me; it had waited for me between the covers, waited to become a kind of sign, a secret pact between Kosti and me. If I came back later and looked it up again, it would no longer be there, having already served its purpose.

These were foolish thoughts, and as soon as they emerged I was filled with doubts. Perhaps the Mervas in the atlas wasn't Kosti's Mervas at all. His Mervas probably wasn't in any atlas whatsoever. And even if this was the Mervas Kosti had referred to, nothing indicated that he'd be there. Or that he ever set foot there. That was what the grinding doubts in my head were saying.

I nevertheless searched the actual map to see where the place was. It was up north, way up north, in the middle of nowhere. *Mervas*, the map said, but there was no dot or square to indicate the place or reveal anything about it, just the six letters and something that appeared to be a road or possibly just a trail leading to it. I kept searching. At least Mervas was now a place in the world. Whatever it represented, it was a message from Kosti to me. Whether he really was there didn't matter, I told myself. The important thing was that he'd sent me the name of this place after more than twenty years of silence. This place was marked on a map, it already carried the possibility of a story, even though it hadn't been described as a village or mountain or with any other cartographic symbols used on a map. That was just as he'd written in his letter. Mervas was farther away than anything else; you couldn't get any farther away.

Finally, after searching several encyclopedias and books about various municipalities, I found additional information in an older encyclopedia. *Mervas*, it said, *former mining community in L., the mine closed in 1951, community abandoned and all buildings dismantled and removed in 1953.*

So it was a nonexistent place. A former place. A ghost town. That's where Kosti was. With the name of this place, he'd shaken and roused me from the sleep I'd allowed my life to sink into. I read the brief text several times, feeling oddly upset. It was somehow completely impossible for me to rationally and sensibly grasp these simple facts. I saw nothing but messages: hidden, intricate, subtle messages. Am I this shut-down mining town? I asked myself. If so, what did this mean: *all buildings dismantled and removed*? Was this *former mining community* our relationship, our love affair?

I tried to make sense of it but only became increasingly confused. It really wasn't so surprising that Kosti was in a nonexistent place, considering that he was an archaeologist. I used to be an archaeologist too, once. Now I wasn't anything, I'd been on disability, as it's called, ever since I was locked up in the dark city during my time away from the world. Suddenly, I was struck by the notion that perhaps Kosti knew something about all that. The fact that Mervas was an actual mining town made my heart flutter with terror. "The Salt Mine" had been the patients' name for the ward where I'd been locked up. I tried not to think about this, not to let my mind return there. After all, Kosti was an archaeologist, and it was entirely expected that he'd be in a place like Mervas, an existent but nonetheless shut-down and removed *former* place.

Our love, or our love affair, lasted for seven, almost eight years. Our meeting at the university was all to Kosti's credit. We increasingly happened to sit next to one another during lectures and seminars. He always seemed to end up by my side. I was suspicious and grumpy. In my opinion, men only wanted one thing, and that thing was dirty and repulsive. But his smile was so open, he casually said *hi*, and sank down in the seat next to mine, his body boyishly relaxed and exuding a faint scent, a dry and grassy scent, which distracted me during the lectures. I was both attracted to and frightened by that scent. Before we became friends and started talking to each other, I sat stiff as a board next to him and avoided looking in his direction even when he spoke to me. But I couldn't avoid his scent. Discreet yet clearly distinct, it surrounded him like a cloud, and I noticed how it did something to me, it sort of prepared a place for him inside me and made me expect his presence.

I truly never thought that another person would want anything to do with me. I'd always been alone, even in my own family; I was somehow the child outside the pack, the odd, lonely sibling viewed as "Daddy's girl" in a home where Daddy was a monster. It was like collaborating with the Germans in Norway during the war. Or like being a German whore. Thus I was excluded from the pack right from the start. I felt as if I carried something around, a weight, a plague, an unforgivable guilt, and it tormented me; not so much while I was by myself, but as soon as I was among other people. That's when I felt it; I was a burden. Just as you can never get away from yourself, you can never get away from your family. You're steeped in its influence, sometimes only a little, sometimes a lot. My family had made me into someone who stayed away. I was ashamed;

not just of being Daddy's girl, but also because of all the despicable things my siblings and I had witnessed and suffered. We'd been made accomplices to something we couldn't comprehend, and in addition to that shame, I've also always felt ashamed of being ashamed. Nothing on earth is as steadfast as shame. I've been thinking that if when I get old I feel like embroidering one of those wall hangings with a saying on it, it will say in red cross-stitching: *A debt can be repaid, but shame lasts forever.* Because that's how it is.

Despite all this, Kosti stubbornly wanted to be close to me. He kept sitting down next to me and talking to me. My sharp edges and grumpiness never affected him. He often laughed at me, but I was more surprised and amazed than hurt by it. It was as if he freed me from everything difficult, released me from shame and set me free.

Since that time I have realized this: everything catches up with you eventually: your past, your fate, your sentence. It took seven, almost eight years. That's how long my respite lasted. Sometimes I watch nature films on television. The moments before the lion catches up with the gazelle, the fox with the hare, the wolverine with the reindeer, those are the glowing moments, the moments of life's ultimate freedom. Then come the claws, the teeth, the fall. It's as if I already knew it, as if it were etched into me; I was the prey.

I remained sitting by the big table in the library with the map open in front of me. I tried to conjure up an image of Kosti and the way he might look now. I even tried to picture him laughing up there in Mervas, if that's where he was. I wanted to know why he'd written to me, what had made him want to contact me after all these years. Could it be, I asked myself, almost petrified, could he be waiting for me?

Looking back at my life, I know I've ruined it. Sometimes I wake up at dawn to something that closely resembles a vision. I see what life is. With piercing clarity, I see it as the unbelievable miracle it is: a tiny bubble, shining in different colors, sailing all alone through a vast, encompassing darkness. It's a bubble in time, a brief moment on a frequency quickly rushing past, a scene performed only for an instant. I awaken at dawn as if touched, as if burnt by this unfathomable truth. The next moment, I am filled with pain, a sorrow so powerful that it almost suffocates me. It's not simply that I haven't made the most of my life; I have also done violence to it.

Perhaps that's why I've decided to go to Mervas. In some way, I already knew this when I went to the library to look through the atlases. I'm going to sell everything I can, get rid of my furniture, the apartment, all my possessions. Then I'm leaving. I'm going to enter my life, enter the shiny bubble. That will be my penance.

November 29

Mom died giving birth to my youngest brother, and with that, you might say our family was dissolved. The baby boy was put up for adoption, despite Dad's protests, and the rest of us were placed with various friends and relatives. We weren't even allowed to attend Mom's funeral; the adults thought it would be too traumatic. It was better for us kids if everyone pretended that nothing had happened. I ended up with Dad's mother, together with my sister, who is two years older. Our three younger siblings were taken in by Mom's brothers, and they didn't want anything to do with Dad's family after what had happened, so I didn't see the twins or my little sister again until all of us were grown.

I became obsessively organized in an effort to keep everything in place. Nothing could be changed or go wrong; my sense of order in the world depended on it. I was twelve years old and every paper clip and eraser had its own assigned place in my desk drawers. I devoted myself entirely to studying and being good and completed all my assignments, even the extra ones, according to instruction. I was so careful with my brand-new schoolbooks that I hardly dared open them; I sort of peeked in between the pages through a three-inch opening. I was also reluctant to erase anything in my pristine notebooks. Instead, I tried to train myself always to write correctly from the start. Everything in my life had to be at once transparent and impeccable; there could be nothing to remark upon or criticize. This applied to my hair, my thoughts, my schoolwork, my desk drawers, and my feelings; everything had to fit into the same mold of perfection. In a diary from this period, I'd made lists of "reasons to be happy" and "reasons to be sad." I found the old diaries a few years ago when I cleaned out the upper cupboards in the hallway, and they made for miserable reading, which definitely belonged in the second category. Getting a perfect score on a math test was an obvious reason to be happy, but being second best or one point off was a reason to be sad. Overall, the reasons for being happy were few and rather vague: "nice weather," "cabbage pudding for dinner," "funny movies." There were more reasons for being sad or upset, and they were more detailed. "A letter from Dad" was high on that list, along with "praise from people I don't respect" and "stomachache," which meant I was having my period. I'd also written down "nightmares," but that was in parentheses, and later crossed out. Dreams weren't reliable. Neither was my body.

I regarded my body as a repulsive feral animal, and I tried to keep it at a distance. I still remember how I tried different ways of moving so I wouldn't feel my clothes against it; I couldn't stand feeling how my body stuck to me and sort of groped me. When my classmates arranged dance parties, I never went; dancing seemed gross, and I wrote a lot about that in my diaries. Girls who wore makeup, miniskirts, or tight clothes I secretly considered sluts. If one of those girls addressed me in school, I turned away demonstratively. It was as if they carried a plague, those who danced and wore makeup and dressed up, a corporeal plague I had to stay away from at all costs.

It was harder to protect myself from my own body, and the plague that it spread. I got my period early, at twelve, when I'd just arrived at my grandmother's, and the smell rising from my blood-soaked pad was enough for me to understand that everything originating in the lower regions of my body was appalling. To be neat and live secluded in the ordered world I'd created around myself was my protection. Black water lapped underneath that order, deep as an abyss one could fall headlong into. My life was either/or, order or chaos, so I had to be very stern and careful, and for years I kept refining my sense of order, all through high school. At twenty, I was firmly determined to live the rest of my life as a virgin. I would devote my life to study and perhaps later in life some big research project; marriage and children were something I never even considered. I was twenty-two when I met Kosti, and he just laughed at me when I explained my position. It wasn't a scornful or mean laugh, but glittering, almost loving. I was completely disarmed and felt incredibly relieved.

"You," he said. "You want to be loved. From all the way in here."

He pushed his index finger deep into my belly button and I stood still as if paralyzed, drinking the joy that bubbled like sparkling water from his eyes. Later on, when we'd known each other for a while, he teased me and asked if I wasn't willing to share my virginity with him.

"Just a tiny bit," he pleaded, "so I can become a virgin too!"

He didn't call me Marta, but Mart, and he said it with a pronounced "r" and a soft "t." You might say that he made me into Mart, that he came and opened and released me from Marta.

We studied archaeology together. In the summers, we excavated and traveled. We were inseparable. Sometimes we got upset with each other and argued, sometimes we had nothing to talk about, but we were always together, we were meant to be together; it seemed our connectedness would never end. It was during the last year of our relationship that I became obsessed with the idea of having a child. I wanted a child with Kosti, immediately. But he didn't, not yet.

"I want to turn thirty first," he said. "Then we'll have kids, plenty of kids."

Even though he didn't quite understand it, Kosti probably knew that our conflict was about something besides having children. It was the old fear, the fear of the plague that had risen inside me again. I wanted to protect myself against something, but I didn't know what it was, and I grew desperate. We lost sight of each other, perhaps also got scared of each other; at any rate we were suddenly moving in different directions. I was twenty-nine, and so was Kosti. He went on the yearlong trip to the Orkney Islands by himself. It was a trip we'd planned to take together.

"I'm not coming with you unless you're willing to at least try to have a child with me," I'd said. Because I still didn't think he was capable of leaving me and I didn't want to accept the seriousness of what had come between us: my life, my entire life.

He left. And a year later, the boy was born. Kosti didn't contact me that entire time. Not until he had returned from his trip did he call, and I told him about the boy. After that, he wrote and called a few more times, more and more rarely. Then, silence. I never went looking for him. He'd moved to another part of the country, that's all I knew. The way I looked at things then, I viewed him as having mortally wounded me, first and foremost by not being the father of, I almost want to say, our child. He'd left me and my life now belonged to the boy, now it was the two of us who were inseparable. I often found myself thinking pointless things, such as that if Kosti had been the father of my child, he would have been healthy. It was as if my mind refused to complete the thought that if Kosti had been the father, the boy wouldn't have existed at all. I knew, technically, that the boy had a father, and that Kosti wasn't him. But I never truly accepted that reality. The way I saw it, the boy was fatherless. That was Kosti's betrayal of both of us.

December 2

I'd become a mother, but my child was locked away in the hospital and couldn't come home with me; he cried incessantly day and
night; he almost wasn't a real child, and I was his mother. That's
how it was. For one year my boy lived in the hospital and I was there
with him, sleeping on a cot in his room the first few months, living inside his crying as if inside a cave of hoarse, exhausted crying. Back then, no other world existed except for the one contained
inside the hospital's red bricks. I had to subscribe to that world and
its routines, routines that made the days so similar they eventually seemed
like one, like a simple, rhythmic pattern repeated again and again, a ticking without variation that kept the world going. No suffering or pain can
resist being swallowed by a hospital's regulations and stubborn reasoning.
An ingenious protective net of cleanliness and restraint is perpetually
suspended over the abyss. It wasn't until I was locked up inside this alien
order that I began to understand what the pedantic rhythm in my own life
had been about. You can think of order as a spine or a corset; that's how
I used to think about it myself. Now I know that its primary purpose isn't
to hold things together. It is to shut things out, to repel and shut things
out. That's what it's for.

I sat there with my child, enclosed by the hospital's vast order, surrounded by the small cell filled with my tears and the face of my child. I felt as if I were traveling on board a spaceship drifting off course through the universe. All connections to my old life – my history, my memories, my sense of context – had been severed. After three months, the doctors convinced me to move back home. I had to get some sleep, they said. I had to get my life back in order.

"I don't have a life without the boy," I said. "I have no life to take care of."

Nevertheless, I staggered out of the hospital and my sister came to bring me home. She'd been watering my plants, opening my mail, and paying my bills while I was gone. Now she led me into town, led me out under the incredible, enormous sky, and all the way to my small apartment, where my old life lay wrapped up, waiting for me. She'd prepared a welcome-home dinner and bought wine. On the table was a bouquet of Easter lilies, and outside the kitchen window, the leaves were opening on the birch. At once, I became aware that it was spring, late spring. I sank down on a chair by the table and stared out at the birch, massive tears welling up inside me. A gray mountain of tears.

"I'm like the boy," I moaned. "I just cry and cry – "

I tried to laugh a little, but it wasn't possible. Instead, my laugh turned into a bawl, a long bawl growing out of my mouth like a plant, the stem of a plant. I couldn't breathe; it felt as if my bawling would suffocate me. It was a sea of sound filling every part of me; I ran from the table, threw myself on the balcony door, and tore it open. My sister was right behind me, yelling and pounding her fists against my back; she held me, and I felt the cramping subside; I could breathe again.

"It hurts so much," I sobbed into my sister's hair. "Everything hurts so much. I'm crashing to the ground. Every bone in my body is breaking."

We let go of each other quickly, my sister and I. We weren't used to that kind of intimacy; it made us uncomfortable.

From then on, I slept at home most nights. I made myself watch television and read the paper, tried to pretend that this was me, that this was my life. Outside, summer was in full bloom, but I took no part in it. There is a particular kind of white-hot anguish, a daylight anguish that can scorch you, make you thin and transparent like rice paper. That's how I felt that summer. Seeing a wasp could mortify me to the point that I ran all the way home and crawled into bed struggling with the white-hot feeling. I scarcely had the courage to live.

Some days I couldn't make myself visit the boy. I'd remain sitting in the kitchen or the hallway for hours, incapable of moving. Sometimes I called my sister.

"I can't make myself visit him," I whispered into the phone.

Then she'd come over and accompany me to the hospital. Or take me to the bus stop. If she set me in motion, I could keep going on my own.

But there were other obstacles, obstacles that had to be overcome. There was the very smell of the hospital. You had to submit to it. When I'd lived there, I must have gotten used to it; I guess I'd reeked of it myself. But now, the distinctive odor bothered me. It filled me with its order and regime. It's a very particular smell, and you can sense it most inside the bathrooms, an odd brew of cleanliness and decay, topped off with rubber and ointments. Shivering, I'd allow myself to be filled with it once more, even though I'd rather have escaped. But I'd make it through the corridors and up to the ward. Stopping at the nurses' reception desk, I could already hear the boy crying in his room, his tired, cracked cries mixing with the music box endlessly chiming "London Bridge Is Falling Down." I'd take a deep breath, and go in to see the nurse, if she was there.

"Did he have a – "

"Oh no, everything's fine."

I didn't want to utter the word *seizure*. It was one of those harmful words no one was allowed to say. The nurses knew about it too, they made deliberate and complex efforts to avoid saying it. But the doctors used the word dispassionately, as if they were trying to normalize it.

"We can't say for sure if he's been damaged by the latest series of seizures," they'd say.

What to them was simply a field of knowledge was for me nothing but suffering: penetrating anxiety, and deep terror. Most of the time it seemed as if they couldn't see the great difference between them and me: to me, the boy's condition would never be an interesting subject; it was a nightmare.

Most difficult was his crying. It never ceased; it was a saw slowly cutting through time. It was sawing through the bones, every bone in his body, and every bone in mine. The seconds got stuck in its path, bone shards, sharp as spears. His crying was hoarse but loud, somehow finding its strength, its source, somewhere inside his small infant body.

In the beginning, when I asked if he was in pain, no one could give me a straight answer. They said he wasn't supposed to be in pain. That there was no obvious reason he would be in pain. That they'd done everything they could so he wouldn't feel any pain.

"If that's the case, why is he crying?" I asked.

But with time, I learned not to ask. I learned to sit next to his crying, to watch over it and hold his tormented little face under my gaze so that he'd be sure to know I'd never leave him, ever. I wanted his pain to become my pain, wanted to share this unbearable, difficult, unfair thing with him, it was to become my fate too; I'd make room for it in my life.

---

"I think I know why he's crying," I said once, during morning rounds.

"Is that so," the ward doctor said, turning away from his colleagues for a moment to look at me.

"I think he's mourning his life," I said. "He's crying out of grief."

An awkward silence followed, and I immediately regretted what I'd said.

"Well, that's possible," the doctor said. "I guess you could look at it that way."

The boy had brown hair and brown eyes. A nod, a greeting from the nonexistent father. Actually, it was a beautiful little face, in my eyes perfect. But with time this face more and more came to be obliterated. Little by little, it drowned in its own absence. During the first months, when I sat and more or less stamped his face within me, it was as if I understood that I had to bear witness to its existence, that I had to recognize its every detail and every last expression because later I would have to live with only the memory of having seen it, the memory of its existence. And then I would know that beneath the expressionless, vacant mask that illness had set on him, another face lay hidden, a wonderfully beautiful, living face had existed but was invisible.

Eventually, they operated on the boy and he stopped crying. The twitching in his arm also disappeared. Now he was a still and silent bundle. My child was a still and silent bundle with human eyes, and I could finally bring him home.

I often think about the boy these days. Ever since Kosti's letter, he has occupied my thoughts. I think I was afraid of remembering before. But that didn't protect me; it probably made me even more scared. I was walking around as if asleep, and all the animals on the savannah know that sleepwalkers are easy prey. I know that the boy is one of the roads leading into the dark city, one of the roads that dissolve in there. I'm now walking down that path trying to recall my time with him, to remember how it was when I took him home. I was a mother then, because I gave up everything else in my life for him; I can see that now, afterward.

But he wasn't like other toddlers, my child. He never learned to sit or stand, never laughed or flailed his arms around when I leaned over him in his crib. He just was; he lived only through that strangely solitary gaze. His presence was without gesture or sign; it was more like a condition, a state of soul. And I allowed myself to disappear into it. I lived with him in a space that cannot be measured in minutes or years. It was a kind of eternity, like timelessness inside time itself. Sometimes, I can discern the shadow specter that used to be me, moving around in this apartment where I still live, moving around the child who was trapped inside his own body and refused to participate in life. I still have a few objects and a couple of photographs to confirm the actual existence of that period of time. But I don't know; it's as if they're not proof enough.

Incomprehensibly slowly, the boy did change. He developed and regressed at the same time. As his face increasingly faded and seemed to grow remote, he finally learned how to sit, and even to stand up. At pre-school age, he could almost walk. With great effort, he could force first one, then the other leg forward, take one step, two steps, three. But most of the time, he was falling. He fell and hurt himself and cried, then fell again. But I still thought I caught a glimpse of triumph in his eyes when he took his first steps on his own. It was a victory over a heavy, unyielding world, one I think he experienced consciously.

Actually, the first six, seven years with the boy weren't so difficult. When he was still a small child, I could keep him on my lap, rock him, and sing him songs. When he was sad, I could comfort him, at least part of the time, and the few words he learned were enough for us; they were the important words in a world we shared. And for us, there was no other world.

As soon as we got to move home, what had been a despicable hospital transformed into a good and safe place. All our visits there comforted me, the checkups and the follow-ups, because in the hospital, people regarded my child as almost normal; they played with him and joked around, they even called him by his name. In some way, they created a context where I became a mother among mothers and he a child among children. Doctors, physical therapists, radiology staff, and nurses – they all related to the boy as if he was real, and they made it possible for me to feel the same way. He was a boy, a little boy. Sebastian. Yes, his name was Sebastian. I don't know why it's so hard for me to think of his name; I always think about him as the boy. Perhaps names carry some kind of promise, and I'd named him Sebastian in the maternity ward, when he'd just been born. This was before I knew anything about his illness, I lay gazing at his amazing little face and thought: Your name is Sebastian.

When he was around three years old, he spent the days in a special needs day-care center, because I had to go back to work. I found a part-time position in a museum and was completely content there even though what I really wanted to do was research and excavations. I was responsible for the museum's collections, and if nothing else, it gave me the opportunity to use my organizational skills. The job was a healthy kind of normality, a kind of plaster, filling in all the cracks and holes in my life.

No one could predict what would happen with the boy when the time came, but around twelve, thirteen, he entered puberty. Suddenly, pimples covered his increasingly swollen nose, and the smell of sweat that surrounded him was acrid, like that of a feral animal. He also started growing rapidly. His feet, his hands, his whole body grew. I felt he was growing away from me; it became very complicated to be his mother. I was quickly transformed into a hollow mother cocoon that had become too small and stayed on the floor with his toys. I felt insufficient, but I knew I had to keep going. He was completely helpless, and his dependency didn't decrease when he became sexually mature. Rather the opposite. Suddenly, powerful urges that his half-sleeping body would never be able to satisfy raged through his body with full force, yet out of his reach.

It happened so fast. One day, he was a head taller than I. But when he walked, I had to support him. Crutches and walkers were too complicated for his uncontrollable body. Sitting still so much of the time and taking so many medications had also made him bulky; he was incredibly heavy and I barely had the strength to hold him upright. He could pronounce about ten words that I understood, and he had a series of gestures and sounds I'd learned to interpret. Sometimes he knew when he had to go to the bathroom, but most of the time, he didn't notice the signals his body gave him, didn't know what to do with them. It was as if a vast no-man's-land separated his consciousness from his body. He was lonely somehow, inside his own body. When he was younger, I'd been both his consciousness and his body. Now everything was becoming much more difficult. I couldn't assist him enough; he'd been trapped by his corporeal limitations.

I know they would have found a place for him in a home for the severely handicapped if only I had asked. But I never did; I never even inquired about the possibility. The boy and I had a pact. He was my lot in this world, my duty. He was assigned to me, and I to him.

Mom sits on the couch, her face patchy red from being beaten, her arms and hands scratched. She stares vacantly before her. Her frizzy hair looks like foam around her narrow, tired face.

On the floor is a mess of books, knickknacks, potted plants, pillows, clothes, and toys. The window curtains are torn into shreds.

The only sound in the apartment is that of children crying. The twin boys, who haven't yet learned how to stay away and keep silent, have been spanked with the rug beater. Next to Mom on the couch is my older sister. She puts her arm around Mom's stiff shoulders, and cries softly. I'm sitting on the floor with my little sister on my lap. I am not crying.

It is evening. Dad has been visiting the "Exception," as he calls the place.

"Have you finally learned what a strayed wife's home looks like?" his thin lips ask, still trembling with rage, before he leaves us.

I go out to the kitchen. He has opened all the cupboards and swept all the glass and china from the shelves. First, I gather up anything that's not broken or just slightly chipped and put it on the table. Then I sweep the floor and put the shards in a piece of newspaper. Finally, I mop until no trace of broken glass remains on the floor.

December 15

A cold insight woke me early this morning, long before dawn. I suddenly realized it would be completely crazy to travel to Mervas. I must have been living in some kind of dreamworld since I got Kosti's letter. I now feel ashamed of my own childishness, my madness. If those thoughts of Mervas appear again, I'm going to call the psychiatric ward and ask them to lock me up for a while.

Kosti is calling me again. Once more, he wants to throw me off course. But this time I'm going to keep going in my own tracks; this time I'm not going to listen to his siren calls. I am old. I feel my life will soon be over. I don't have the strength to live anymore; I've already been through too much. For years, I've struggled to accept the truth of that fact.

Growing old has been much harder than I'd imagined. Since I've never cared very much about the way I look, the way other women do, I didn't think I'd care particularly about things like wrinkles, getting a potbelly, and gray hair. But I did. It was devastating. My body fell apart and suddenly became my great source of sorrow. It became a wound that wouldn't heal, but instead grew larger and deeper. To undress and sink into the bathtub became painful; I tried not to let my gaze linger anywhere on my body, but I could still see, of course. The fine, pathetic pubic hair, which insisted on growing on my thighs instead of covering the mound, disgusted me. So too did the patchy, blue-veined legs. It was all too sad. Like being forced to watch your house fall into decay without being able to do anything about it. Like watching a plant wither. At once, my whole life seemed so wasted, as if I'd neglected to live it while I could. It hurt me so much to realize this. It caused me so much agony that I started hiding like a young girl when I had to undress. The very air wasn't allowed to see me, neither was the light of day, barely even darkness – I had to hide my nudity at all costs. For some time, things went so far I started neglecting my hygiene; it's quite difficult to keep clean without removing your clothes, so I hardly ever washed. Nor did I buy any new clothes, and I let my hair grow unkempt. Finally, I could sense that I smelled bad. I could smell it in my bed, and when I returned to the apartment after being out, my smell greeted me, stale and sickly sweet, putrefied. That's when I made up my mind. I was supposed to be old. I was allowed to grow old. It was natural and obvious and nothing to grieve over, I just had to adjust to the new order of things. The threads of life had simply grown thinner, the weave had become sparse and brittle, and that's what was visible in my body, that's what my body was trying to tell me. The notion was almost liberating. I decided to allow life to run its course and told myself to stop hoping and fantasizing, to stop dreaming about change, mercy, and love – all those things that human beings cling to and refuse to let go. Now I was going to devote myself to concluding things, to folding up and sealing the past.

In the last year, that's how I've adjusted my thinking. In some ways, I have had to conquer myself. But I'm taking care of myself again. I buy clothes, take baths, and cut my nails. You have to be able to tolerate your own life. Day after day, you have to carry yourself through it.

Kosti's letter disturbed me. For the second time, he's trying to disrupt my sense of order. Now I know. There's nothing for me in Mervas. And I don't want to see Kosti again. As far as I see it, he could just as well be dead. I mean, I haven't known whether he was alive or not for the past fifteen, twenty years. He probably doesn't know any more about my life after we parted than I do of his. He doesn't know about the boy's death. Most likely, he hasn't a clue about the repercussions our love affair had on my life. How it threw me off course and into chaos.

When life has become too torturous, when it has been infused with pain the way water can be infused with salt, you no longer want anyone to witness it. You don't want to be seen. No, true suffering doesn't want to be witnessed. It hurts too much. That's why I'm content being as lonely as I am. No one can see me. I'm glad that ever since the boy's death, the contact with my sister has been limited to a few phone calls a year. I don't want Kosti to see me. Only idiots think it's necessary to drag everything to the surface for show. Many things can only heal in darkness, out of sight. If they can ever heal at all.

December 21

For the first few weeks after Kosti left for the Orkney Islands, I was at war with myself. The struggle between the Red forces, which wanted to swallow all pride and be reconciled at all costs, and the White forces, which refused to bend, was constant and ruthless. I was becoming an increasingly ravaged battlefield. Weeks could go by when I didn't get out of bed in the mornings. I thought like the child I still was: He thinks I'll come anyway. But I'll show him. I'll show him who he's dealing with. I'm not going to come crawling back to him like a sorry dog and lick his fingers.

I wanted to be strong and proud. To defend my honor and let the White forces win the battle.

When the war was over and the Red forces had been conquered, I was powerless for a long time. A kind of fatigue that closely resembled an illness paralyzed me. I didn't have the energy to think. If I even got close to completing a thought, I felt as if drugged with exhaustion. But I sensed, yes, I could sort of hear, that beneath this huge fatigue, my rage was whimpering. If I'd had the capacity to listen more attentively, I would have heard something else besides the rage. I would have heard my fear squeak. And the lamentation, the lamentation from someone who had just lost everything.

But it was my rage that one night led me to put makeup on my face and dress up in a way I never used to, that fortified me with a couple of glasses of wine and sent me out to explore the city's bars. There, I soon got quite drunk since I wasn't used to drinking, good girl that I'd always been. So when the man whose name I still do not know started caressing my buttocks during our dance, I pressed myself harder to him.

When we arrived at his small, messy dorm room, I found out that he was a couple of years younger than I. To my surprise, I also noticed that he was both shy and insecure in my company. As I'd always thought I'd be the one to be shy and insecure in a situation like this, I started feeling something I'd like to call a power high. I felt strangely cruel.

We sat on two chairs opposite each other, drinking instant coffee, and my irritation grew with each sip I took. In various ways, I tried insinuating that I hadn't come home with him just to have coffee and chat, but he pretended not to hear my hints. Instead, I could tell from his face that he felt pushed further and further into a state of confusion and gloom. It wasn't that he didn't want me. I could tell that he wanted me, my callous eyes could see that. But he didn't have the nerve.

I felt in some way clinically evil, and I enjoyed it. I didn't feel sorry for him at all. Instead, I regarded him with a passionate severity. He was struggling to free himself like the wingless fly a little girl had placed on an anthill. Now that I had become someone I was not, now that I'd started the game, he too had to join. I wasn't going to let him bail out like a kid when the game gets too scary, to bail out whining: *I don't want to play anymore.*

When we'd finished our coffee and nothing happened and the clock was ticking toward three-thirty in the morning, I went and lay down on his bed. I was on my back, looking at him, and he sat glued to his chair, looking back miserably.

I could whip him, I thought, almost lustily. The notion caught me by surprise, I usually did not think or feel such things. At the same time, there was something oddly familiar about the feeling, an echo from far away. A quivering tension.

"Now that you dragged me to your place, you damned well better do something about it," I hissed at last.

"I'm sorry," he said.

He finally came to me. We turned out the light and our clothes flew across the room. Naked in the dark, we turned into small animals. After a while, our hands and tongues and lips made all the insecurity and contempt vanish. We had sex over and over again until dawn became morning.

Waking up hungover the next day and realizing I wasn't lying next to Kosti but a complete stranger, I felt terrible. I didn't want to look at him and I didn't want to know his name. I didn't want to see him wake up and I didn't want to exchange a word with him ever again. I didn't even want to get close to thinking of what had happened during the night; I just wanted to erase it from my memory. So I carefully snuck out of bed and gathered my clothes. I quickly showered him off my genitals, got dressed, and padded out.

Since then, I have never been with a man. And I doubt it will happen again. I don't know why I say "doubt" – it will never happen again.

A few weeks later, I realized that my period had decided not to come. My relationship with Kosti was now irrevocably over. I had no thought of an abortion. I was going to show Kosti how serious my desire to have children was. To have a child now. How much he'd hurt me when he'd forced me to let our child be fathered by someone else. How badly he had wronged the child.

December 22

An odd thing happened upon receiving Kosti's letter. I didn't want it to happen, but I suddenly saw myself as part of a story. And it was about me, about Marta.

Everything inside me resists it, but it is as if the story presses itself against me and I can't get away. It is as if the story itself is going to carry me. Out of this. At the same time, it has to move straight through me, like a child who needs to be born and on its way out ruthlessly opens up all the closed inner portals. The mother may burst from pain, but that doesn't matter. The child has to come out.

The arrival of Kosti's letter bothered me. It forced me out on a marsh, and when I try to find my way back to solid ground, I realize that the only way to go is straight through the memories, as if they were planks laid out for me to walk on. In some strange way, I think telling my story will bring me back to solid ground. The problem is that I've never enjoyed reminiscing. I have never devoted myself to telling or even cultivating my memories as some people do. I've never told anyone about my childhood, not a single person, not even myself. The reason for that is simple. There hasn't been anything to tell, there hasn't been a story. There have only been scraps. Bits and pieces.

Until now, I've lived according to my own order and taken refuge in it. I've been able to decide that this week I'm going to read this or that book and focus on this thing or the other. Because even though it has been a long time since I worked within my profession, I've continued doing a little research on my own. In this way, I've been able to live inside my own mind. I've looked for books and articles, read dissertations and research reports.

But for the last few weeks, my thoughts have constantly been elsewhere. Like flocks of birds, they've lifted from the pages and flown away. And my thoughts have not been fluffy daydreams or memories of the boy. No, they've been busy telling a story, assembling, comparing, sorting, and memorizing. I have been forced to realize there is an order to this also, but a different kind of order than what I'm accustomed to. It has even struck me that there are similarities between the writing I've begun and an archaeological excavation. The carefulness. You have to be so incredibly careful with the things you find down there. They may for example be positioned in a specific order in relation to one another that mustn't be changed. Or they may be fragile and crumble at the slightest touch. A sudden shift of the hand (or the brush, or the pen), and the entire story could literally dissolve into dust.

You can have what appears to be a disorganized collection of bits and pieces. But the truth is that the position of each shard of vessel, its exact place in relation to the other pieces, is just as much a part of the puzzle as the shard itself. What I think, especially since I began to write, is this: every piece is part of the puzzle, of a story.

It is quite easy to lie without being a liar. All you need is a slight imbalance. Or the wrong internal order. One little bump in the road can overturn your cart, as the saying goes. One small, insignificant imbalance somewhere in the story may one day topple over and grow into a different story. You don't have be false to lie; I actually think you can make up events and still tell the truth. Lying isn't so much about a lack of truth but rather a lack of meticulousness and devotion. It is not about disturbing the sensitive balancing act that truth represents, but rather recognizing this frail order and sensing it inside you, just as the tightrope walker senses every muscle and tendon in her body before she steps out on the rope.

Something I've been thinking about is that for long periods of time, I've been imagining that Kosti was dead. It's been a small, hard, tugging notion inside me. He could actually be dead without my knowing it. It's been frightening to think about this. Like walking around with someone dead inside you. Secretly harboring a dead body.

Other parts of me have tried to convince me that I'd know if he were dead. That something inside me would change. This change would be noticeable but very slight, like when a petal falls from a flower and floats to the ground. There'd be a difference.

But that first thought has still continued to tug at me, no matter how hard I've tried to push it out of my mind.

You wouldn't notice his death, it tells me. His death would alter less inside you than a flower petal. Reality is prosaic, it has no connection to the hereafter, the thought insists triumphantly.

I realized it was one of those thoughts that are out to get you, that want to crush you, want to shrivel the world. But now I know. He exists. He called me from somewhere. Through my life, through the ruins among which I've been moving, he called me. And that thought tugs at me harder than any other. It's a thought that could turn the world on its head.

December 25

My dad had one passion. He wanted to populate the world with his off-spring. At the very least, he wanted as many children as it's possible to conceive in a monogamous marriage. The way he saw it, it was Mom's duty to assist him in this mission. She was meant to give birth to all of his children. That was the sole reason for her existence.

After Mom's third pregnancy, from which came twins, the doctors warned her that another pregnancy would put her health at serious risk and suggested sterilization. When Dad heard this, he became so enraged that he pressed a knife against her throat and said he would kill both her and us kids if she went through with the procedure. She was soon pregnant again.

Dad wanted to prove something with his big and healthy brood. It wasn't simply to show that he was a virile and capable man. No, the main thing his offspring were supposed to prove by their quality and intel-ligence was something the world had so far neglected to acknowledge: that Dad was a genius.

But Mom's fourth pregnancy became very complicated. She had to stay in the hospital for a month after the delivery. When she finally came home, Dad would spew his venom upon her at every turn.

"A woman who can't bear strong and healthy children is utterly useless," he declared at the kitchen table. "In the old days, women could give birth to twelve, fifteen children without suffering any damage. But the modern world has ruined motherhood. The sloppy lifestyle, the doctors' coddling, the entire medical profession is false. Listen to me, modern women are spoiled. But I'll tell you this, she can do it if she wants to!"

The color rose on his cheeks in a frightening way as he spoke, or rather, lectured. My dad didn't speak, he lectured.

"Women who give birth," he proclaimed, and gestured theatrically. "Women who give birth! There are no words, I repeat, no words as grand and beautiful as these!"

At first, he lowered his voice when he continued speaking.

"But modern women don't want to give birth. They think it hurts too much. Ouch, ouch, it hurts! They can no longer stand pain. Can't stand the pain that has sanctified women for thousands of years. Do you understand? Do you understand what I'm saying, children? Do you understand how important this is for me, for you, for the future? I want you to understand what I mean when I tell you that your mother is useless. She's a useless woman because out of some kind of stubbornness, she refuses to bring children into this world. This makes her subhuman; genetically, she's garbage! And this is my wife. Your mother."

I don't understand how Mother could stay quiet. How she could remain where she was sitting. But she did. When our eyes would meet, I would immediately avert mine. I was so terribly ashamed in front of her; I felt dirty and guilty and deceitful. And her gaze was somehow inquisitive. *Do you believe what this man is saying?* it seemed to ask.

Dad especially liked to lecture at the dinner table. The fact that his lectures often turned into loud, hateful rants of unbridled rage didn't seem to have any effect on his appetite. He shoveled the food into his mouth between sentences, quickly and mechanically. The rest of us sat quietly trying to chew and swallow as best as we could while we carefully observed the characteristic and ill-boding quakes of anger that rippled through his thin body like an electric current.

But it wasn't enough for Dad to hold forth alone in front of a gloomy, silent audience. He wanted both assent and participation. The dinner lectures were part of his educational mission to elevate Mom, and especially us kids, to his level.

"Can you understand this, Marta, that your mother, your own mother sitting there chewing her tough beef stew like a cow chews its cud, do you understand that genetically, she's garbage? Do you grasp the meaning of these words, Marta?"

He always had to turn to me. In his eyes, I was Daddy's girl, and also more gifted than my older sister. He was speaking in a very low voice and his lips were thin and taut like rubber bands. When he lowered his light blue gaze into my wide-open eyes and fixed it there, lashed it there, I hated him so much I wanted him to die. The hate burned inside me like a dry chemical fire.

"Yes, Daddy, I understand."

"Well, then I'd like you to explain to me, and the rest of us, what it is you claim to understand. For example, what does the word *genetic* mean?"

The word "genetic" sounded like the crack of a whip when he said it. I could sense the vibration of the word inside him; it seemed to fill the whole kitchen. If he'd had whiskers, they would have vibrated like those of a cat spotting a small bird.

"Well, Marta. *Genetic?*"

The way he said "well" was forceful like a vise, and I often felt that I could kill him for the way he said it. It was also in conjunction with the word "well" that the rug beater would be brought out and used in explosions of uncontrolled rage. The word "well" was a dam that at any moment could burst from the water pressing against its walls.

"It has . . . it has to do with inheritance," I said. "It means hereditary, it's hereditary."

Animal breeding was one of Dad's special interests. He worked at the Department of Agriculture and specialized in hog breeding. Sometimes, to the relief of the entire family, he had to travel to different parts of the country to inspect selected groups of breeding hogs. It was on one of these occasions that Mom packed up some linens, clothes, some pots and pans, and toys in big boxes. Then an uncle we'd never met before came over and put Mom, the boxes, and us into a Volvo station wagon and took us away. That's how we ended up in the two-room apartment, which Dad later started calling the Exception.

Mom had evidently planned the move for some time, because the apartment was already furnished when we arrived. There was a worn sofa bed and a couple of plain beds, a kitchen table, some chairs and stools, a dresser, and a big brown radio with its green dial eye.

Mom probably hadn't asked her family for help before because she felt ashamed. After all, she'd been lucky to enter a good marriage with a well-educated man from a better family than her own. The way everyone saw it, she ought to be happy and content. The marriage to Dad had distanced her from her family, and as the years went by, the distance kept growing, especially because Dad didn't think Mom's relatives were good enough for him and his children. It was probably the doctors she met in the hospital after my sister's birth who pushed her to get in contact with her family and tell them what was going on. All of us siblings immediately fell in love with our uncle. He was very tall and fat and had lots of amiable lines around his eyes. He constantly made jokes and laughed more

during the move than our dad had done during our entire childhood.
And he was a father too, we found out. There were fathers like him in
the world also.

December 28

It's the Feast of the Holy Innocents today. Outside, it's thawing and suddenly the snow has no resonance or sparkle. All afternoon, I stood in front of the bathroom mirror looking at my face. Looking into it. I was searching for something in it, I don't know what. Perhaps a bit of life, an ounce of longing somewhere in the depth of my eyes. But my face was indecipherable. It expressed everything and nothing. Most of the time it was ugly, but for brief moments it was beautiful. It never ceased to be invasive; painfully, embarrassingly invasive. Like someone who comes to bother you. A stranger at once mysteriously intriguing and revolting. I just stood there, unable to step away from the mirror.

Many artists have been known to paint their own portraits; some become obsessed with it. I can understand why. They're trying to fix on the canvas the one face that always eludes us more than any other. Perhaps our own face isn't really available to us because it eludes us. On the contrary, it turns away from itself and toward others. Way back in the past, when no mirrors existed except for the occasional shaky reflection in a body of water, it was the people surrounding you who became your mirror. They reflected your face back to you, responded to it. I sometimes wonder if people were different back then. You're so alone in front of the mirror, alone with your own perplexing face. Perhaps our faces want to tell us that the person who lives unseen has lost his face. That our faces are there for others, it is a language, perhaps even everyone's primary language.

I've probably lost my face. That's what life has done to me; it has driven me deeper into loneliness. My face has become unreadable, not only to myself but also to everyone who sees me. It has become an extinct language. I thought of Kosti there in front of the mirror. I wondered if he'd be able to give me my face back.

My years with the boy made me think a lot about this, about faces. His great loneliness was hidden precisely because he was missing his own face; he couldn't reach anyone through it, couldn't reach outside himself and was forced to remain inside his own darkness. Like being born without a body, I sometimes thought. A diabolic impossibility. And I, the mother, who finally couldn't endure his loneliness.

I had a terrible dream last night. I dreamt there was a war. My apartment was on fire and I stood on the street outside with a group of other people and together we saw the fire rising against the night sky and enveloping the entire neighborhood in worrying clouds of thick, brown smoke. Soon after this I found myself on a military airfield. It was early dawn. Muddy roads passed between big, depressing sheet-metal hangars. I was filled with an incredible anguish. Groups of soldiers passed me by and harsh voices gave orders all around me, commands, deadly words. Suddenly, Kosti's father came up to me. He was dressed as an officer and he gave me a small piece of paper.

"Go to hangar G," he said sternly. "You're going to the front."

Hangar G, the front. My legs felt weak and I stood there, confused, with my little piece of paper. I didn't know in which direction to go. Then I found myself in a dilapidated locker room, where grim guards dressed me in a uniform and hung weapons, ammunition, and a pack on my back. They pushed me out to a giant hall where soldiers were lined up, and I understood that I'd come to hangar G. I was placed in the first row of soldiers, among those who'd be the first to leave. I'd never felt such intense fear before. When I looked around, I spotted Kosti's father and right behind him stood Kosti, in civilian clothes. They both looked straight at me, and when I screamed that I didn't want to go to the front, Kosti's father appeared and said that I must behave myself, that I had no choice. I had to go to the front and the plane that would take me there was about to take off.


I woke up before boarding the plane. My anxiety was like a spear thrust through me and I was soaked in sweat. When I'd gotten out of bed and had my first cup of coffee, I knew that I had to get myself to Mervas. Not because it was "the front" or to escape "the front" – I wasn't yet in any shape to analyze the dream. It was more of an insight that had come to me, a voice that the night had stripped bare, and this voice knew. I had to go to Mervas. I've known it the entire time; that's how it has to be, that's what has to happen.

December 31

We actually parted as enemies, Kosti and I. There's no other way to describe it. Perhaps love creates in us an obsession of wanting to be loved completely and entirely, into every part of us, every corner of our being. But when I became increasingly determined to drag Kosti into my darkest, worst stinking nooks and crannies, he turned away from me. He immediately became hard and impenetrable. I had crossed a boundary and his otherwise mild demeanor changed, and he became dry and barren and harsh. A stony desert. And he forced me out of his life; there was never a way back. His very words pushed me away. He didn't have to raise his voice, didn't even have to scream. The harsh and dry way he spoke to me was enough. He drove me away from him with those words, out of the apartment, the little dorm room we had shared. That was all it took. I was already crushed.

I slept in my car that night, and the following day I moved to my sister's. I didn't dare return to him; I was afraid to hear that voice. To see the lack of love in his eyes. I couldn't take it, not from him, from Kosti, who had seen me, received me, and renamed me. I was also afraid of being held accountable, of being reminded of the person I didn't want to be, the one I wasn't. To meet myself in meeting him.

We argued that night. It was worse than that; it turned into a scene. But before we started arguing we'd had a really nice dinner together. It was actually our celebration dinner, the last in the apartment. In a few days we were going to the Orkney Islands and before that we had to pack, move out, store our things. This was the last peaceful night at home before the big moving and traveling chaos would begin.

After dinner, we were sipping the last of the wine and fantasizing about the upcoming year we'd spend on Sanday, an island northeast of the Orkney Islands. We talked about the ocean and about the fall and winter storms, about the uninhabited skerries and the megalith burial sites we would study. Everything seemed so incredibly exciting. We hardly dared believe that we would be there in a few days and then stay there an entire year. We were both hopelessly romantic. We described images to each other of how the raging storms in a kind of violent act of love ravaged the flat, rocky islands with their sparse vegetation. Roaring, the storms would press and wail against the tiny houses, which mostly resembled orderly stone cairns. We described how the wind held the island land-scape in its grasp out there, how it scraped and tore at the yellowing grass. The salt would penetrate the cracks in the small cottages, become mortar in the stone walls, and glisten like crystals in the curly wool of the sheep. We could see ourselves there, walking close together through the storm, struggling to stay upright and screaming to each other to be heard over the din from the sea. Finally, we'd have to throw ourselves down on our stomachs and lie there, pressed to the ground, with our lungs completely filled with air while the hard wind kept moving through grass and twigs.

Both of us started glowing as we talked. Everything we mentioned immediately became warm and alive, a hot fluid metal, which we shaped and melted down and reshaped again.

---

"Yes, and even you have to understand this," I suddenly heard myself say. "In a place like that you just have to conceive a baby. I mean that's where you make love to become pregnant!"

Kosti quickly seemed to sober up. He sighed, and his expression became harsh and edgy.

"Dearest Mart, not now. Not again. We decided not to discuss this until after the Orkney Islands. You promised, remember? Right? You promised to wait until I was ready."

It happened so fast. The Orkney Islands drifted away from us and disappeared somewhere far out at sea. And there we were, Kosti and I, sitting opposite each other in the sudden calm, interrupted and lost. It was terribly quiet. The ticking of the battery-powered clock could be heard through the whole apartment: ticktock, ticktock.

I could have done something. For example, I could have gone and fetched the book about the Orkney Islands that we had just bought and said: Okay, let's forget about that for now, let's look at this instead. Or I could have spread the big detailed map on the floor for the hundredth time and said: I'm sorry, we should let it go, it just came out of me, I don't know why. Come here!

Or I could've said that he was right, we had actually decided not to talk about it, we could discuss having children when we returned, and I wouldn't nag about it anymore.

But inside my head, a small voice said: *You* have decided, not the two of us. *You* want to wait; I don't. And I sat there silent, caught up in a strange, eerily quiet anger, which slowly spread inside me and filled me with its shadowy gray demons. I sat completely still and allowed thoughts to rise that I couldn't reverse and didn't want to have. A cruelty was coming from inside me that I couldn't defend myself from.

Kosti didn't do anything to change the gloomy atmosphere that had taken over the room either. An unpleasant smell seemed to have found its way in through the cracks in the windows. The very air between us had changed, but we didn't know what to do to get rid of it. Kosti also remained silent, as if he were waiting for something. It was as if there were a secret director waiting in the wings, manuscript in hand, anticipating the next line. As if everything had already been entered into the great book of life, already decided. All we had to do was fill in the blanks with our voices.

I cleared my throat. The words had to come now, before they killed me; I could feel them inside, insisting I let them out. They had to come out into the light and be destroyed like vampires. Perhaps then they'd be gone forever.

"It's a pity, really, that we're not Catholic," I began, noticing at once that my suppressed anger made my voice vibrate slightly.

Kosti gave me a stern look.

"If we were, we wouldn't even have to discuss the subject of children, we wouldn't have to. We'd just let the children arrive."

"Come on, give it up," I heard Kosti cry out, from somewhere far away, from the other side of the sea.

But I kept going, I had to get into it, it was an old dry wound that I had to scratch and tear at now, until it bled.

"Catholics are really the only ones who dare to speak the truth," I said. "They come right out and say that contraceptives are a sin. That it is a crime, a crime to prevent conception! You have to agree with this at least; they come out and say it and even though I don't think it's a crime against God, it's a crime against nature. It's a crime against mankind, against women, yes, especially women. Oh, I don't think you understand anything at all, we've spoken about this so many times but you've never heard the truth, you've never gotten to hear what I truly think and feel.

You know why? Because you wouldn't understand it. You're lost inside your pretty little world where everyone's just friends and the notion of men and women, instinct and differences almost doesn't exist!"

I was aware of how agitated I sounded, half screaming, as if I were being attacked or held down by someone. As if I were afraid.

"That's why I've never told you what I've felt when we've made love using contraception, without a thought of having children. You wouldn't understand, you who live in your own sweet little fairy-tale world. But I want you to know that I've felt like a whore, like a cheap fucking whore every time you slept with me. And it's you, Kosti – no one else – who's defiled me, who's made me dirty, who's made me feel disgusted with myself, simply because you've denied me the right to be a woman. Do you get it? You've denied me my womanhood!"

Kosti had now demonstratively turned away from me, letting his gaze disappear into the darkness outside the window. It was actually quite odd that he didn't leave the room or at least growl at me to shut up. But this was a one-person show and my words could not be stopped. I was a ditch full of sewage and the messy words gushed out of me.

"Your greatest flaw is that you don't know what a woman is. No, you don't, and you probably don't know what a real man is either. You'd probably shit your pants if you met a real woman; she'd scare you, Kosti, because she's not part of your worldview, she doesn't exist in your pathetic, friendly teddy-bear world where every damned person is so smart and kind it makes me want to throw up. You know, a real woman, she is a mother, first and foremost a mother, and even if men can run around spreading their seed here and there – yes, spread it into the storm on the Orkney Islands, by all means, do that – women are made to carry, you understand, she wants to carry the heavy fruits, she wants to be fertilized and carry, fertilized and carry. You get what I'm saying? She simply doesn't want to be some kind of fuck-buddy and have a good time between the sheets because that's not what it's about! No, she doesn't want to be a worthless tramp, which you seem to want to reduce me to. That's what you make me into when you humiliate me like this; you deny me the right to become a mother, you won't make me feel like a real woman and give me a child even though I've asked for one. It's the most revolting, cruel thing you can do to a woman, and that's what I want you to understand, that's what you have done to me with all your talk about contraceptives and wait until later and all that. That's what you've done to me, that's what you've done – "

Finally, I ran out of words. There was simply nothing more to say and I remember that I felt emptier than I ever had in my entire life. It was as if an army had passed through me, an army that had plundered and burned everything and left nothing behind but bare, scorched earth. The room was once again quiet. It was quiet for a long time. Until Kosti turned to me and looked at me with those eyes in which no love was left.

"Leave," he said. "I want you to leave. I don't want to look at you. I no longer know you."

Feeling completely numb and blank inside, I went out to the hallway and put on my coat. Then, without a word, I left the apartment. All night, I lay folded in the backseat of the car with my eyes open. I couldn't sleep. Couldn't cry. And I remember that it felt terrible that I didn't cry, that I couldn't even cry.

It is a Saturday evening in the apartment we call the Exception. Mom, my older sister, my twin brothers, and I are in the big sitting room drinking tea and listening to the radio. My little sister is asleep in the smaller room, where Mom's bed is.

When someone rings the doorbell around eight-thirty, Mom's eyes get empty and distant. She buttons the lowest button on her muumuu and pulls her hand through her hair.

"Please, Mom, don't open the door," my little brother whispers.

Mom only looks straight ahead. The doorbell rings again, a longer tone this time.

"Take those things away," she says absentmindedly, nodding at the tea tray. It's my task to try to hide things that are easily broken. Fortunately, we no longer have a teapot that we care about. We've been brewing our tea in a regular pot on the stove for the past few months, and that's been fine.

As I'm running to the kitchen with the tray, the pounding on the front door begins. Soon I'll hear Daddy's voice through the mail slot. He usually calls for me, telling me to open the door.

I hide as much of the china as I can in a small space I've discovered behind the kitchen drawers. The teacups don't fit in there, but there's room for tall glasses and coffee cups. We've kept all the plates in the drawer under the stove for some time now.

My hands tremble violently as I put away the glasses. I have to hurry now; pounding and ringing signals echo through the apartment. I carefully put the lower drawer back on its tracks and with some effort push it back into place. When I hear the squeak of the mail slot opening, I run in to the others again.

Mom is standing in the middle of the floor. Her chin quivers almost unnoticeably; the rest of her face is taut. Her back is very straight; in some way she seems large where she stands. My sister quietly comes out of the bedroom, where she has taken the twins.

"Soon the neighbors will call the police," Mom whispers.

It happened once before. I don't think Mom had ever been more ashamed. The police officer told her that in the future, we had to handle our family business without disturbing the neighbors. He didn't want to hear any more complaints about "gypsy behavior" from our building. We ought to be ashamed and behave like everyone else. Mom stood there with her head bent, her face bright red. Dad had quickly disappeared.

"Marta!" he calls, his voice shrill with rage. "Come here immediately!"

He said my name hard and fast, made it sound like the crack of a whip. That's why I've never liked my own name. It sounds beautiful in English, and in Finnish too. But in regular Swedish it sounds as though someone has slapped you in the face twice; I still think so. Kosti called me Mart. I loved him for that. He came up with it himself too; I didn't have to ask him.

Mom gives me a look I've seen before. My knees are shaking and my skin stings when I stumble out to his voice in the hallway. I have to be the one who lets him in. Once again, I have to open the door and look into the terrifying face that is simultaneously rigid and dissolving.

As soon as I've cracked the door open, he forces it wide open and gives me a hard push so I fall backward onto the shoes under the clothing rack. He shuts the door with almost unnatural care; it makes me think of a lizard, some kind of reptile. With no apparent transition, he could always move from rest to immediate attack. He's already reached Mom. I hear him calling her names, hear the sounds of him beating her, and I don't want to see it but I have to, I have to. My older sister is in the bedroom with our younger siblings, trying to calm them down. They're sobbing. Someone has to stay and witness this. If I close my eyes or try to hide, I'm abandoning Mom and then I can't protect her with my gaze. In some odd way I have to when I wanted to close my eyes, when they closed even though I didn't want them to, I forced them open with my thumbs. I have to protect Dad with my gaze too, because he can't be left alone in this situation either.

God wants you to see this, said something in my head.

As a child, I believed in God even though both Mom and Dad called it superstition. I prayed to him every night before going to sleep, but no one knew except for my oldest sister.

"Dear God, make Daddy be good and make sure all children have food to eat. Let there be no more wars."

I didn't have to say it aloud; God couldn't hear my voice, he heard my heart. I tried to speak to him with my heart. I tried to explain this to my sister but she never quite understood.

"The heart doesn't have a mouth that can speak," she said.

"The heart *is* a mouth," I said. "Another *kind* of mouth."

After Mom died and my sister and I moved into our grandmother's, when I entered puberty, I killed my own faith in God. I started to despise it; I didn't want it. In the years that followed, I was angrily antireligious and spoke like Mom and Dad about superstition. I agreed with Marx about religion being the "opiate of the masses."

Now I don't know what I believe. Except that my heart is mute, even petrified. Sometimes I wonder why there wouldn't be a God when so many other seemingly impossible and unthinkable things exist. Life is so mysterious and I miss my heart, which has lost its strength. The heart is pure, they say. And I actually believe that, I'm almost sure it's true.

I've put on my shoes and through the doorway I see Dad, who is out of his mind with anger, attacking Mom.

"Bitch!" he pants, trying to keep her head still by grabbing her hair in his fist while he hits her.

"You think a legally married wife can run away from her own husband? You think you own his children? You think you can take the children away from their own father? I'll teach you! I'll teach you how such a wife should be treated. I'll show you, you sly, hypocritical bitch in heat! I'll break you in until you can neither sit nor stand!" Mom is half-prostrate, bent over on the couch, and Dad is standing over her beating her rhythmically, synchronizing the blows with his words.

"Marta!" he yells suddenly. "Bring me the carpet beater!"

"Children!" he then screams. "Come out of the bedroom right now!"

The bedroom door slowly slides open. My sister is standing there, pale and tense, with the twins close by her side.

"Aren't you even going to say hello to your father when he comes to visit?" He spits out the words. "Aren't you? Aren't you going to say hello?"

"Yes," my sister whispers. "Good evening, Dad."

I'm standing slightly to the side behind him with the awful carpet beater in my hand. I'm so terrified it's as if I were standing in a highly charged electrical power field.

"And you?" he snarls at me. "Lost your tongue?"

I have lost it. I try to speak, but no sound comes from my lips; my tongue is like a piece of bark in my mouth.

"You naughty child!" he screams, and tears the carpet beater from me. He gives me a few blows on the legs with the handle.

I gasp from the pain and swallow several times.

"Good evening," I blurt out.

I can't say "Dad." It's impossible.

But this evening is apparently about Mom. She, not the children, is the one who will be disciplined.

"Sit down, children," he says, in an unexpectedly friendly voice. "You see, I want you to know what a family father must do to a woman who has run away, and who also refuses to bring children into this world. Sit down!"

We sit down on the floor, as far away as we can, and now we see how Dad with his free right hand gives Mom a few more slaps in the face while his left hand gets a better grip on her hair. Mom whimpers, it's a drawn-out sound; she's whimpering something and I can finally hear what she's saying.

"Don't let the children see . . . don't let the children see . . . don't let the children see," she repeats indistinctly.

"Silence! They'll see. They're going to see what you're worth. They're going to see who their mother really is underneath this robe. They'll learn how a bitch like you should be treated."

He pulls at her clothes and finally gets her garter belt to slide up until it sits like a belt around her belly while her blouse is inside out, covering her face and head. The words are still streaming out of her mouth, she's half-crying and her voice is shrill and we hear her repeat:

"Don't let the children see . . . don't let the children see . . . don't let the children see . . ."

She struggles and fights back in a way we've never seen her do when Dad has hit her. But this is different. He's never undressed her before, and now he also begins to whip her with the carpet beater, on her legs, wherever he can reach.

"Now shut up and be still, or I'll tie you up the way you bind a sow," he pants between the blows.

Then he forces her onto her stomach and I hear her sob and cry while the carpet beater hits her buttocks and thighs.

My youngest sister, who was only about one at this time, comes crying from the bedroom. She totters over to my sister and curls up next to her. This makes Dad pause for a moment.

"Turn off the ceiling light," he orders. "Turn off all the lights!"

We do as he says. At once, the small apartment is filled with darkness and suddenly everyone's breathing can be heard. Our shallow, terrified breathing, my little sister's sobs, Mom's soundless tears, and above all and over everything else, Dad's panting, growing deeper. He has stopped beating her and in the dimness he and Mom look like one body there on the couch.

"What is Daddy doing now?" one of my brothers asks when the sounds and movements from the couch turn increasingly strange.

"Hush, hush," I tell him, and my sister gets him to stay quiet. After this, the five of us sit motionless in the dark, letting everything happen. I join my hands as in prayer, but they're cramping and I can't pray; my heart feels paralyzed and I'm afraid of everything I don't understand. Let it end, is all I can think. Let it end.

Dad groans. He groans again, louder. Then everything grows silent. Completely silent. It's as if everything that's alive has suddenly escaped from the apartment, as if nothing were left but the darkness and the occasional sounds from outside; a car starting, a door slamming, the sound of steps against asphalt.

Eventually, we hear Dad getting up and straightening his clothes. His white underwear glints like the sliver of a moon through the darkness. He clears his throat.

"You can turn the lights back on," he says in a calm and steady voice. "The husband has fulfilled his duty. The degenerate sow got what she deserved."

The room turns blindingly bright. Mom tries to pull her top back down with one hand, while the other gropes around her as if she's searching for something. My older sister rushes toward the muumuu that has ended up on the floor, but Dad grabs her wrist and stops her from giving it to Mom.

"Behold your mother," he says, and gestures dramatically at her where she sits half-naked on the couch.

After this, he forces us to get in line and go up to him one after the other and kiss him good night on the lips and say:

"Good night, Father dear."

Right before he leaves us, he slams his heels together and bursts out: "Order has been established."

But Mom's gaze moves straight through the walls. It rises from her beaten, black and blue swollen face and the room explodes.

One day when I went to the hospital to see the boy a few weeks after his operation, the nurse at the reception desk cheerfully told me that Grandfather was there to visit.

I just stared at her.

"Grandfather," I said incredulously, as if I didn't know what the word meant, as if it were as complicated to figure out as who somebody's "partner" or "sister-in-law" was.

"You're saying my father's in there?" I asked.

The nurse laughed.

"Yes, I suppose so. From your looks, it's obvious you're related. Gosh, I didn't do anything wrong now, did I?"

I said nothing, only shook my head a little and took a few steps out of her sight. At first, I felt empty inside, as if I'd lost my moorings and were drifting. Then my feelings swelled up inside me, hatred and anger mixed with an incomprehensible joy, and I was mortified. Would my dad be sitting in there with the boy? Was that even possible? I hadn't been in touch with my father for ages. He had, however, been meticulously faithful in sending Christmas and birthday greetings every year, but I'd rarely responded to his little messages, particularly not when he'd been careless enough to write things like "Daddy's own girl" or "my own favorite" on them. Those words made me feel things that would prevent me from sending Christmas greetings to him for years to come.

I walked slowly down the corridor. Underneath my coat I felt cold, as if I'd caught a fever, and my heart was pounding in my ears. It felt impossible that I could walk into the room and he'd be there, with the boy. What right does he have, I thought angrily, what right does he have to burst in here? Over and over I asked myself: *What right does he have?* With each step I repeated the question, probably because I was actually quite confused and because so many other words and voices were crowding inside me, complicated words, dangerous voices. By asking myself this question, I could keep the other voices at bay.

I paused when I reached the boy's room. The walls facing the corridor were made of glass, and even though they were covered by drapes, you could look into the rooms through the openings between them. I stood still for a moment, barely breathing, and then I leaned forward a little and peeked through an opening right where the boy's room began. I had to close my eyes quickly, because Dad was sitting in there, it really was him, and the sight of his familiar figure burned me like fire. I opened my eyes and took another look. Yes, he was sitting there; I saw him from the side and he was an old man, I could see he had some white hair on his head and he was thinner, more bent, as if he had shrunk. "You have to look," something inside me said when I wanted to close my eyes again. At once, my whole past fell upon me; the memory moved like a hard gust through my entire nervous system. And I looked.

He was seated next to the bed, leaning forward, holding the boy's hand. As far as I could see, his eyes were closed, while the boy was lying still in his crib with his eyes wide open, gazing at his grandfather's face. I stood breathless outside the pane of glass and watched them, waiting for a motion, for something to happen. But nothing changed, nothing happened in there. Dad kept his eyes closed and held the boy's hand and they were both completely still. It was like a *tableau vivant*, and I couldn't help myself, I felt calm; it was a beautiful and strange image. It was also quite incomprehensible. Why had Dad traveled here, and who had told him about the boy? It couldn't be my older sister; since Mom had died, she hadn't spoken to Dad once. It really made no difference who'd told him; what I couldn't understand was that he'd ventured to visit my boy. That he'd traveled here to visit a child who was neither healthy nor normal.

I couldn't make myself enter the room. It wasn't only the unpleasant-ness or fear of meeting him. I also didn't want to interrupt the picture, to upset it, because there was something peaceful about it, something beautiful. It affected me somehow, like a miracle-making icon. My father's slightly lifted face expressed a simple tenderness that I'd never seen before. I sensed more than I could see that he felt a deep con-centration; something in his face flowed through his arm to his fingers, which clasped the boy's small hand. The boy seemed focused too; his gaze exuded a pure and direct presence steadily directed at my father.

The tears running down my cheeks brought me back to the present moment. Annoyed, I wiped my face with the sleeve of my jacket and looked around, suddenly aware that anyone could pass by and see me. I didn't want to stand there crying in the corridor. What I ought to do was go and ask my father what he was doing here with my son. What right did he have to be here, and why was he sitting there like an idiot with his eyes closed, holding the boy's hand? But I couldn't. I just wiped away my tears and stood there. I didn't know what to do. You can't love a father like mine. It's not possible.

At last, Dad opened his eyes; he probably felt he was being watched.

———

I quickly moved away from the window and half-ran to the bathroom. I closed the door behind me without a sound and locked it, but I didn't turn on the light. Instead, I sat in the dark with my head in my hands and allowed everything that wanted to tear me apart to rise to the surface. Tear me into pieces, I thought, tear me into a million different pieces. I can't hold myself together anymore.

I sat there for a long time before I turned on the light. Then I carefully washed my hands and face before I opened the door and went out again, firmly determined to go in to the boy whether my father was there or not.

But he'd already left. Perhaps there was something of him left in the room when I entered it; a scent, a presence, I couldn't quite tell. Later, I thought that maybe everything I'd seen that day might have been a dream. I could have asked the nurse about it, but I didn't. It felt best if it remained a dream vision.

The next time I found an envelope with my dad's handwriting on the hallway floor underneath the mail slot, my first impulse was to throw it away. But instead, I put it unread in the drawer where I kept all my letters. Not until many years later, when I learned from my brother that Dad was dying of cancer, did I read it.

"Dearest Marta," it began. "I don't want you to be angry with your old father if he were to tell you that he has visited your son in the hospital without asking your permission."

It was a real letter this time, not just a greeting on a note card.

"But I did it because I'd heard that your little boy was very sick. In a lecture on the radio, I'd heard the theory that a person can transfer their strength and health to another human being if only they want it wholeheartedly and if they hold the other's hand and put all their energy into it when they meet. I don't want you to think that your father has gone and lost his wits. Dear Marta, I wanted so much for your son to heal that I was willing to try everything! Perhaps this may seem to you like I'm trying to redeem myself too late, but I want my girl to know that her father deeply regrets the ill deeds he exposed his beloved family to. He understands fully that he can never be forgiven for such acts. But I want you to know, Marta, that I regret what I did, every day, all the time." It would have been simpler if I'd been able to hate him completely and fully, if I'd been able to feel nothing but hate, the way my sister did. Nor did she ever understand what God had whispered in my ear when we were young – that I had to look, that I had to be a witness. That's why I went to see Dad on his deathbed and sat with him for a few hours. I'm not entirely sure if he could see me, but I think he knew that I was there even though he lacked the strength to show it.

It was difficult to sit with him. I couldn't make myself touch him. He died later that night, when I was on my way home on the train. My brother called and told me, the one brother who for some reason had kept in touch with Dad all those years.

April 11

It's been a long time since I wrote anything. But now I've terminated the lease on my apartment. I know it's crazy and I can barely admit to myself what I'm doing, but I think I have to respond to life in some way; it has held me accountable and I have to say something, do something, prove I take it seriously. Inside my head a voice whispers: *You're allowed to die. You can do it*. And I'm trying to understand these cryptic words, the strong sense of relief they awaken in me. Suddenly, I'm no longer anxious. Life doesn't have to be preserved at all costs. But it has to be lived, that's what the words are telling me. I've found the door that leads to life, and to my surprise, I've discovered that it's marked Death. You're going to die, the voice tells me; therefore, you're allowed to live.

With respect to practical things, I'm trying to be systematic. I'm going to sell or give away most of what I own. I'll use the money to buy a car, a used but robust car that I can sleep in if I need to. I'm going to pack some books and papers, letters, photographs, and other memorabilia in the big, coffinlike trunk I inherited from Dad. I will have to ask my sister to keep it in her attic for a while. That's the hardest part of all these preparations. We've barely communicated the last few years, mostly just called on each other's birthdays. But I have to tell her I'm leaving, even if

I won't specify exactly where I'm going, or why. I'm not going to mention Kosti. Maybe I'll say that I'm moving to the countryside, that I've rented a cottage somewhere, something like that. I know how she'll look at me when we meet, how her eyes will move across my face while she thinks: My, she's old. Or: Has she gone crazy again?

I can imagine how I will respond, with a stern gaze and controlled expression: No, I'm not going crazy; I just want you to keep my trunk for me.

When I've left, she'll call some of our siblings that she's in touch with and tell them:

"Marta's moving. Somewhere in the countryside."

Then they'll talk about me. I'm not entirely sure why, but the mere thought makes me squirm; the fact that they'll talk about me, mention my name, kind of touch me in my absence. As if by doing so they touched me intimately, touched something that ought to be kept hidden, that no one should deal with except me. My name. My life. My shame. It's that creature inside me that doesn't want to be seen. The one that wants to live without a face. I don't want anyone to touch or poke that creature.

I'm not really leaving because of Kosti. It's quite plausible he has already left Mervas. But if there's anything in my life that isn't broken and ruined, I want to find it and take care of it before I die. Last year, I turned fifty. Many people die in their fifties. It could happen to me. Perhaps I have to be taken off track to find my way, to find what's right.

This was the feeling I had: that I was running out of time, that it was flowing away from me like blood from a wound. I felt this in the rooms where I had to stay, where I was locked up because my life was fused to the boy's life. I had to stay where his muteness became my muteness and his immobility became my immobility. In this state, time was bleeding away from me; everything froze and stood still, became a cast of what life should be. It was like living without ever having been born.

I stood looking out the window. It seems to me now I stood there for years. The world outside was also frozen. The protected old fir trees on the grassy slope looked like ancient creatures that had gotten lost in the landscape. They were giant lizards and I was waiting for the moment when they'd break the spell of their inertia and take off. Sometimes when the wind blew hard through the treetops, I could feel a peculiar anticipation. Now, now, soon . . .

But the world didn't move. It was exact and unyielding and didn't deviate an inch from its set course. I'd watch cars come and go; they occasionally left their places in the rows of parked cars, but they always returned obediently – red, white, orange, and blue cars. Seasons passed through trees and bushes, snow melted and snow fell, the leaf from a potted plant fell off, and dust settled on the windowsill. Time was moving relentlessly, always at work; it flowed and rippled like water under the blanket of snow, emptying itself. And the world stood still and allowed itself to be emptied, a still life, a skeleton, a meticulously assembled sculpture of dead time. I was part of that that sculpture, strapped to the great stationary wheel of frozen time. I had the slow gnawing sensation that this wasn't where my life was. Somewhere beyond my reach, life was ongoing, my own life as well as everyone else's. But I wasn't invited to participate in it. I wouldn't even have been invited to my own wedding, if I'd had one.

There is a quality of precision in life, an incorruptible order that cannot be made relative. Life is relentless the same way death is. Everyone has a place in their own story with a myriad of threads running forward and backward, upward and downward, like a web. If you want to cut yourself loose, you have to cut yourself off from who you are. You can't just switch your life for another. The details of your existence may be unbearable, but they are nevertheless wrapped up neatly and connected to each other like the threads of the web. Now, afterward, I can acknowledge what I couldn't see while it was happening: that those last few years with the boy were awful. If I'd been a better person, made differently, I would have asked for help; I would have screamed for help the way I raged and demanded it the day the boy was born and they tried to take him away from me. But I couldn't speak. Dumbstruck, I believed that the boy was my life, that without him close to me, neither of us would survive. He was as helpless as a fetus, a big, shapeless fetus I nourished with my blood. I lived with him as if I were pregnant and waiting for him to finally be born. That's how it was.

Yet I believe in free will. Theoretically, I think that even someone like me could have chosen a different fate for the boy and me. But a person's will has many layers, and some of them may be buried under the earth. I believe in free will, but I also believe in darkness. In the great darkness that in all directions surrounds the tiny sphere of light where we live our lives. I think the dark is real even when we're lost inside it, even when we can't see it.

Spring is approaching. Suddenly, light has blown into the evenings and filled them, made them swell and lengthen. I heard such passionate birdsong from a tree behind the parking lot the other afternoon that I thought at least a hundred little birds were sitting among the branches singing and chirping. But no matter how I looked, I couldn't see a single one. It was as if the birches themselves, still without leaves, were resounding with song.

I went to the boy's grave today. A white wagtail sat on his tombstone, balancing, so I stayed a few yards away as not to frighten it.

"Welcome, white wagtail," I whispered. "Are you bringing me a message?"

I couldn't help myself. It was as if the boy had taken the shape of the bird and was addressing me, touching me. It had been a long time since I had visited his grave. I didn't even go to the cemetery on All Saints' Day.

When I walked up to the grave, the wagtail flew away, but it didn't go far. The whole time I was there, it stayed close, nosily walking around in the grass behind the tombstone. It stayed with me, somehow.

Several crocuses had already come up in the wet, muddy ground, still just buds, but I could see which ones would be yellow and which would become purple. I had brought tulips in different colors and placed them in a vase, which I pushed into the soil.

I don't usually smoke, but I've made it my habit to smoke a cigarette when I visit the boy's grave. When I've arranged things, flowers and such,

I crouch down, light a cigarette, and smoke. It's my way to stay with time, to just sit with time for a little while and let it exist.

Kosti was a smoker. He mostly smoked a pipe, but sometimes cigarettes too. He taught me how to do it. I remember how he used to sit down on a rock or a tree stump while we were doing an excavation and he'd just disappear for a bit, into the clouds of smoke he created. Sometimes I'd walk over to him and ask him for a hit. We'd sit together for a while, in the space the smoke created.

When I'd smoked for a while, I pressed the still glowing cigarette butt into the ground as hard as I could. Down into the boy's soil. Into the soil that was the boy.

"I can see you," I whispered before I got up to leave. "I will carry you with me, all the way to Mervas!"

After I'd walked away some distance, I turned around and saw that the wagtail had returned to the top of the boy's tombstone. This filled me with gratitude. Perhaps also with hope.

I was the one who'd killed the boy. I did it. Sometimes when I stumble around in the dark city that is my life, I find myself standing again in the room where it happened. And it happens again inside the darkness, I do it again and again, and it will never end.

It was on his birthday; on the day he turned fourteen. My sister arranged for the tombstone later. It says *Sebastian*, and then the dates show his birthday and the day of his death to be the same. At first, it tormented me so much, that the exact dates had to be carved into the stone too; why wasn't it enough just to mention the years?

I wasn't present at his funeral. I was wedged into a darkness that had frozen into stone. I was inside that darkness for many years, locked inside my deed. Locked in a moment.

II

She finally arrived, Marta did, but not in Mervas. Instead, she came to a small village called Deep Tarn, which really wasn't much of a village since there was only one farm there. Nevertheless, that's where the sometimes winding, sometimes dead-straight gravel roads finally led her. To Deep Tarn. None of the roads she'd tried to follow led to Mervas. No matter how she'd tried, none of them had let her in, had ever let her reach it by the right road. She was close to Mervas, not there, but she knew it must be close.

It was the third day of her journey and she'd been driving around in the county she hoped was the right one ever since morning. She'd driven on bigger roads and small side roads, she'd passed bogs and empty open places and come into sparse, rolling pine forests with a tarn in every little hollow. She'd come out on clear-cut areas where devastation spread as far as the eye could see; she'd crossed creeks and driven along bubbling, rushing rivers in a seemingly endless wilderness. One single car was all she'd seen the entire day, a grayish black car that had swerved through the gravel and disappeared in a cloud of dust before she had the time to decide whether it was good or bad to meet another person in a place so devoid of human life.

She was often so afraid she wanted to cry. Sometimes her legs shook so much it was hard to accelerate. The car jerked forward as in fear through the endless woods. She was leaning forward, her hands anxiously clutching the wheel, not wanting to admit what she'd gotten herself into.

She was afraid, and her insecurity only grew the farther into this landscape she went. Everything was alien and indecipherable; she was a complete stranger in the landscape that surrounded her for miles and miles on all sides, she knew nothing about the things she saw, knew nothing about the rules that must govern in places like this. Sometimes, when the road brought her to a high point and she could look out over the trees, she saw that the place she'd come to was endless. She was imprisoned by that endlessness, captive in a network of nameless gravel roads, and the farther she drove, the more lost she got.

Once, she stopped and stepped out of the car to look at the scenery. A long, low mountain range stretched in every direction. The silence was immense. It was as if for the first time she understood the true meaning of silence, the complete absence of sound. The silence pressed against her ears the way compact darkness can press against your eyes. She stood listening to the pounding inside her head while her eyes were gliding over the vast landscape, and in awe she let her gaze move gently along the shapes of the giant mountains that continued for as far as she could see. There were lakes out there too, calm, silvery gray sparks in the silence. Everything around her stayed where it was; it was there, it simply existed. Through her fear, she realized that this silence was a powerful language, a mighty voice louder than anything else. She'd never felt as terrifyingly small as she now did. She felt she could be obliterated here, the vastness of the landscape could dissolve her with just a whiff of wind; she'd have to beg the small, dim-green pines for mercy. At the same time, she felt herself growing in the vastness, felt herself being pulled and stretched and filled by it. It was as if she could contain it, could contain everything around her.

While she stood there on the slope and let the silence and the vistas fill her up, the wind casually moved closer from the mountains on the other side of the valley. It traveled down into the woods below and kept moving from one forest to the next, from tree to tree, up toward the place where she stood. A sound grew slowly through the silence, slowly sort of snuck up on it, as if tiptoeing. The sound was at first slight and scattered but then grew denser and gathered in a herd of whispers and sighs. Suddenly, it was as if she were standing in the middle of an enormous chorus. All the forests in the landscape took several deep breaths and then they sang. Upper and lower voices washed over her, high and low notes like big boulders rolled through the silence, but the gale itself, the wind, still hadn't touched her, she could see it tearing through the crowns of the trees below her for a long time before it suddenly reached her, grabbing hold of her hair.

She ran to the car and sat inside it, gasping for breath. She had absorbed the performance outside feeling a mixture of pleasure and terror, she had stood as if petrified listening and watching and now she wanted to scream out loud, now she felt that the immensity of everything threatened to suffocate her. It would make her explode if she wasn't allowed to use her own voice to resist and scream that she was here too, she existed and wasn't going to let herself be obliterated by something huge, she was here and had the right to be.

But Marta didn't scream. She sat for a while, letting her breathing slow down. Then she started the car and kept driving. She'd stopped looking at the map on the seat next to her; it wasn't right. No map could capture

83

or describe a place like this, she thought. She drove without direction, and it was already evening. She was so worked up that when she saw a small, beat-up, pale yellow sign with the words *Deep Tarn, 4 km,* she immediately turned onto the road simply because it had a name, because there were letters.

It was a very bad road, narrow and full of potholes. In some places, large, sharp rocks poked through the gravel like sharks' teeth, and in other places, it was so wet and muddy that she had to press the gas hard and swerve forward. Here and there, thin saplings grew out of big holes in the road, as out of the holes of a lake covered in ice. She regretted that she'd taken this road, but it was too late now, there was no place to turn around. Fear kept her going, a compact wall of anxiety that had pressed out of her the sheer will to survive. She had to keep moving along this road, there was no other option.

When she spotted a small barn, propped up among big stones in a spacious and tall gathering of pines, she felt an almost overwhelming gratitude. The small, simple barn appeared to her a symbol of gentleness and goodness. Some of her tension subsided, something softer revealed itself among everything that was harsh and rigid. Then the woods opened up a little more and there was a clearing with lots of open sky above, a house and a couple of barns, little lodges and sheds and *lavvus.* Some buildings were on the edge of the sparse forest, others among the trees. Some were right on the boundary between the woods and the meadow opening up behind it all. The meadow, with its yellowed last-year's grass and two small barns in the middle, seemed so friendly, surrounding the entire area with its light.

Marta turned off the engine some distance away from the hamlet. This too might be a ghost town, inhabited only by its own memories.

She wasn't sure if she preferred a farm where someone lived or one that was empty; both alternatives seemed equally frightening. But there was something about the way the houses were so beautifully placed around her. She felt a touch of longing for a home, and this was almost like coming home. She felt that she could be here, maybe she could rest here overnight and then, the next day, she'd look at the maps with a little more focus, and find the right road up to Mervas.

It was at that moment the dog appeared. A ragged, gray, wildly barking projectile came running along the road as if it were a missile someone had aimed at Marta's car. When it reached her, it proceeded to run around the car in circles, all the while barking loudly and ceaselessly. Marta grabbed the steering wheel; she wanted to leave, didn't want to sit here confined by a barking dog. But the dog moved so quickly around the car, in an instant it seemed to be everywhere, and she sat there squeezing the wheel until her knuckles turned white, helplessly watching the animal dutifully jumping around the car, barking all her thoughts to pieces. Her feeling of unease soon turned to panic. *No one may pass here, no one*, she thought the dog was barking. *Soon my master will come, my master*, she heard. *And he'll shoot you with his gun, his gun.*

"Shut up!" she screamed in falsetto to the dog. "Get away from here!"

But the dog only seemed to get excited by her voice. With a growl, it curled its upper lip and bared its teeth and Marta didn't want to see any more. She leaned forward over the steering wheel and pounded her head against it, pounded and pounded. The thoughts were screaming in her head. *I'm too old*, they screamed, *I can't do this, can't handle things like this, I'm a fool*, they screamed, *a fool, I want to go home, I don't want to do this anymore, don't want to, I'm a fool and I want to go home.*

She was pounding her head against the wheel so frenetically that she didn't notice that the dog gradually grew quiet and that someone was insistently knocking on the window. No, she didn't even notice that someone was standing out there looking at her. It took a while before she became aware of the sound of knocking over her own pounding. At last, she calmed down and looked up, taken aback.

A man was leaning forward, peering through the glass with surprise. Beside him sat the dog looking obedient and good. The man gestured to her to do something, open the door, roll down the window, speak to him, anything. She rolled down the window a bit. But she couldn't find anything to say. She just looked at him through her confusion, and he looked back. He had an old hat on his head, which he pushed back a little. His eyes were shining; they were blue and gleaming strongly like lamps, like lighthouses.

"Did you get scared?" he asked at last. "I mean, did the dog scare you?"

He placed a hand on the dog's head while he studied Marta carefully.

"Not at all," she said foolishly.

"Okay," he said. "You didn't get scared. Well," he continued, drawing out the words and clearing his throat, "I thought my dog here scared you and that's why you . . ."

He nodded at the steering wheel, but didn't say anything.

"I was on my way to Mervas," Marta said. "I got lost. Or rather, I couldn't find it."

He stared at her for a moment.

"I see," he said, emphasizing each word. "I see. You're going to Mervas, you say." He pushed the hat farther back on his head. Then he smiled.

"Well, you were lucky to come to Deep Tarn instead!" he said with gusto, straightening himself. "You know, in Mervas," he continued, "there's nothing. Absolutely nothing. And what might happen to be there, no one wants to know about."

He was silent for a while and looked away, past her. "Are you from there?" he asked.

Marta shook her head.

"I didn't think so," he said. "But there are those who were. And they want to go there and see the place." He laughed. "The only problem is: there's nothing to see in Mervas! Nothing! There's nothing in Mervas but blueberries, we always say. And bears. There are bears in Mervas."

Marta listened to what the man was saying as if under a spell. The entire time, he spoke in a very loud voice. It was almost as if he were yelling. Or as if he were making a speech. And he had a thick accent; he didn't say "bear" but "beear" or even "bearn." She couldn't stop watching him. There was so much life in this man, more than she could recall ever having seen in anyone.

Yet he was older than she was, probably almost seventy.

"Yeah, well," he said, straightening up again. "Now that you've ended up here in Deep Tarn, you might as well step out of the car and have some coffee. You drink coffee, don't you?"

"Certainly. Thank you," Marta said.

She glanced at the dog and the man smiled a little again.

"Just come on out," he said. "No need to be scared of Tasso, not at all. He's a damned good hunting dog, that is all. And he's always on alert!"

Marta had to support herself against the car as soon as she stepped out. Her numb legs felt dead underneath her; she thought they wouldn't carry her.

"I've been driving all day," she said apologetically.

He drew in some air between his front teeth. Then he took her hand.

"Arnold," he said.

"Marta," she answered.

Perhaps it was for real, she wasn't quite sure, but she followed close behind the man with the shining eyes. They were heading for the residence about fifty yards away. The present moment suddenly had a tinge of fragility. She couldn't rely on it; it seemed that at any time it could spill onto the ground where she walked and disappear forever. Nor did she know if what she saw was entirely clear, if she saw it in the right context. The little courtyard she now moved across – didn't she recognize it from a dream, from a very different kind of dream? She shivered. She'd said only yes, she did drink coffee, and that wasn't really very much to say. Most people drink coffee, if only to be polite. She supposed it was possible that anyone could step into a house and get the vague feeling they'd been there before, perhaps in a dream or through a book, or in the distant past of childhood. The man ahead of her walked with such determination, with long, easy steps. He didn't even turn around to make sure she was still there; he knew she was. His entire being watched with those luminous eyes and he didn't doubt for a moment that she wanted to come and have coffee with him. Marta got it into her head that she had somehow taken a step in the wrong direction, that she'd taken one step to the side and slid into something she did not recognize, one tiny faux pas that had brought her into other worlds, other orders. It struck her that this had already begun that day in the library back home, when she found

Mervas in the atlas. That's when the first false step took place. It was impossible to change that now, to undo what was done. This is what everything had turned into; it wasn't what she'd previously decided but where she helplessly found herself. Here. She was here; she was actually following the man up ahead. She knew she was here, a strangely new feeling.

Just as she placed her foot on the landing by the front door she noticed the birdsong, and it was decidedly real. It rose from every treetop and every shrub, from the sky and from the ground so that she was closely surrounded by tones, submerged in a bath of bird voices. Only then did the man turn around to look at her, making sure she was there. He then turned his gaze to the vista below the house, toward the mountain curling its back away from them toward the sky, which was bright even though it was evening.

"Yes," was all he said as he looked at her again.

After this, he slid through the door, which was half-open, and she followed him uncertainly. Two steps through the vestibule, the kitchen was on the left, and its door was open.

"We've got a visitor," the man called with a loud voice as he stepped over the threshold.

Relieved, Marta discovered a woman standing by the stove. She was short and had frizzy gray hair and wore a greenish wool sweater that went down to her knees.

"Well, I can see that," the woman said in a soft voice. She smiled a little at Marta. "I saw you coming," she said, nodding at one of the three windows. Marta's car was out there, left in the middle of the road as if it were still on its way to the house.

The woman poured some coffee onto the lid of the pot, and then poured it back.

"Sit down now," she said. "I'm Lilldolly of Deep Tarn and we don't have guests here very often."

She had set the table with two cups and saucers, bread, butter, and cheese. She poured the steaming hot coffee and returned to the stove.

"Well, I'll have my coffee over here," she said. "I share neither table nor bed with Arnold over there, even though I'm married to him," she added with a wink, and chuckled.

"No, that's right," Arnold muttered. "One's been shown to the gate, or whatever it is people say."

He gave Marta a mischievous glance and slurped some of his coffee.

"Now, have some cheese and bread," Lilldolly said from over by the stove. "And drink your coffee."

After this, silence settled on the kitchen. Marta spread some butter on a piece of the soft bread and cut into the cheese, which looked home-made and had a tart, sharp smell of milk and stable. The dog was curled up in an old armchair in the corner and was looking at them with its head between its paws. Sometimes Marta looked at the dog and sometimes out the window. She didn't dare look at Arnold or Lilldolly. Everything was too quiet; it felt as if they all were naked, as if they didn't have as much as a rag to cover themselves with. No words could protect them. It felt as if time were holding its breath and soon would implode from the effort, from the pressure. But she couldn't break the silence herself; she didn't trust her voice to carry itself. She was also afraid her voice would burst through the room like something foreign, something outside herself.

"You know, Lilldolly, she was on her way to Mervas, this woman, so I told her it was lucky she had come to Deep Tarn instead."

Arnold broke the silence as if it had never existed. As always when he was speaking, the words rang out. It was beautiful, Marta thought. She saw the landscape and the heavens when she heard his voice, it belonged out there in the sea of air, it moved easily through the vast and the spacious.

Lilldolly's voice was low and quiet.

"Was there something you needed to do in Mervas?" she asked softly, and Marta squirmed under her gaze for a while before she figured out what to say.

"No, nothing in particular. I just wanted to see it."

"I see. Well, everything's gone up there," Lilldolly said, without taking her eyes off Marta. "But in the old days it was like going to town when we went to Mervas, there were lots of people, an open-air dance floor and a movie theater and everything. And barracks full of bachelors!"

She laughed her funny little giggle and shot Arnold a playful glance.

"But now there's not a house left up there. Not a single one. That's right. And it's quiet." Lilldolly bent down to get a stick of firewood and put it in the stove.

"All that's left up there is blueberries," Arnold added. "I told her already, nothing but blueberries and bears."

*What about Kosti?* Marta wondered. *Is Kosti still there?*

"They just dismantled the houses and took them away on big trucks. They left the cellars behind, of course, couldn't remove the cellars, so you can see where everything used to be, where the houses were placed along the streets. The cast concrete stairs and the foundations, those're still there."

"There's the little kiosk over by the dance floor," Arnold interjected. "It's still there."

"True, it's still there. The little kiosk by the dance floor is there because the mining company didn't build it. I think it was the young people who put that up, I guess they got permission to do it. Otherwise, no one was allowed to build in Mervas except for the company, that's how it was, people couldn't build anything because nothing was allowed to remain. That was the plan for Mervas. That nothing would be allowed to remain."

Lilldolly was quiet. They all looked out the window at the evening sky. It was growing darker at last; the shadows were long. Marta felt worried. They probably wanted to go to bed soon, as it was already past eleven.

"Well, look at that," Arnold said. "It's night already."

"Yes," Lilldolly said, "there's still a little darkness left for the night." She yawned before she continued: "But what shall we do with our guest? Where shall our guest sleep tonight?"

"*Marta!*" Arnold called out so the whole kitchen resounded. "Her name is Marta!"

"I'll sleep in the car," Marta said quickly. "That's what I do every night."

"No, no, no," Arnold said.

"Out of the question," Lilldolly agreed.

"But . . ."

"No."

"She'll sleep in the *lavvu* with me."

"She won't sleep in the *lavvu* with you when we've got a whole house full of beds!"

"Well, she shouldn't have to sleep alone in the house with an unknown man, that's for sure! She'll sleep in the *lavvu*."

"This woman is so goddamned difficult you almost have to scream for her to understand," Arnold roared, banging his fist against the table so the cups rattled.

Marta stiffened and stared straight into the opposite wall without a thought. Now, was all she thought. Now.

"Watch it, you're scaring her," Lilldolly whispered. "Now she's afraid."

Arnold instantly turned to Marta, pinched her arm lightly, and looked at her with those eyes that were still luminous in the dim evening light.

"You don't actually think I'm scary, do you?" he asked, smiling sweetly, as if at a child. "I've got to," he said in dialect. "I've got to rile her up a bit, this one here, so she knows she was once married to a real man. *Right*, Lilldolly?"

"Very true. Exactly."

She'd been sitting on her stool by the stove the whole time while they were drinking coffee, but now she got up and went over to the table.

"Good night, Arnold," she said, and stroked his hand. "We're going down to sleep in the *lavvu* now, Marta and I."

Long before the arrival of morning, while it was still supposed to be night, the birds began singing. It was the end of May, the time of light. For a few months, the world was coming out of its dark hiding place, radiant and prominent. It was also the time of birds. Everything breathed hot and fast, had light rapid heartbeats, and pulses as quick as moving wings. It was the time of light, of birds, of water; everything was released and rinsed clean and each morning was supposed to be like the very first one, new and translucent blue under thin skin.

There was a smell of water in the air. All of Deep Tarn and the land around it smelled of fresh water. Marta smelled it inside the *lavvu* – the smell of melted and dissolved ice, of soil that water had flowed through. She'd been awake for a while. Inside her sleeping bag on top of the reindeer hide, she was watching the light through the opening in the roof. A good distance away from her, on the other side of the fireplace and kitchen area, Lilldolly was still sleeping deeply, wrapped in her sheets and blankets.

But none of the things outside, the birdsong, the smells, the sound of the wind through the trees that filtered into the *lavvu*, could help Marta get away from herself. She lay listening to her heart beating in her chest like a small, evil, sharp hammer. Arnold and Lilldolly's faces danced in front of her, grotesquely enlarged, sometimes bobbing and floating around as in an aquarium, other times in pulsing flashes. They actually didn't appear threatening; there was nothing angry or dangerous about the faces, but they came so close that they filled her entire field of vision and there was no way she could get rid of them. She could see them, but she couldn't see herself, couldn't see that she had a face just like them. She was nothing but a growing field of darkness. Now, when for the first time in years she was among other people, she found that she had no idea who she was. She lost herself in the company of these people. It was as if she had been blinded by their attention. She stumbled over everything in her way, had to feel the walls to orient herself. It was almost impossible for her to move naturally, or be herself, as we say, because she couldn't see clearly or relate to anything around her.

Over the years, being watched or spoken to had come to feel invasive, like a violation. She'd wrapped layer upon layer of solitude around herself to protect her from a gaze, yet she wasn't exactly sure whose. If she was really honest with herself, she knew it was her own eyes watching her, but she nevertheless kept wrapping that solitude around her; there was nothing else to do.

She tried to sit up a little in the bed to calm down. It can be scary to lie on your back, stretched out and vulnerable. She tried to think of how she'd come to Deep Tarn, how she'd come to Arnold and Lilldolly. This was unknown territory for her, all the trees and the great solitary lakes watching over everything. She contemplated that she'd arrived in a place of still, ancient mountains and loud, winding, gouging rivers and that it was a landscape you couldn't grasp. It was both open and closed, it was din and silence and emptier than anything she could have imagined. This was where she'd come, to this little pocket called Deep Tarn and to the two people who lived here. She tried to think that she was with them now; they'd been here for a long time and they'd let her in, invited her into their world as if that were completely normal. As if her neighbors back home would've opened their door and said: *Just come on in and sit down*, and then just let her be part of their life. As if there were space for her. As if it were possible, and people didn't have to stick to their own schedules and their own lives.

She tried to stay as present and alert as possible. But something kept telling her she'd misunderstood the situation and made a mistake by staying. Arnold and Lilldolly had probably expected her to decline firmly everything they'd offered and to sleep in the car again. They probably expected her to leave for Mervas, or wherever it was she was going, as early as possible in the morning. They'd insisted on her staying only to be polite, all the while hoping she'd say: *No, no thanks, you're so kind but I have to go.*

The strange thing was that she'd never felt that they thought she should have said no and left quickly, and this made everything feel blurry and complicated in the early hours of dawn; their generosity confused her, made her lose track of herself. It would have been easier if she'd been turned away, if they'd sullenly muttered: *Well, you can't stay here, that's for sure.* Or if they'd at least established some firm boundaries so she'd know exactly what was going on. But to just invite her in – it was like falling and sinking into something bottomless. Who was she to receive this hospitality? Did she exist other than as a cast of herself, the remains of something that had long been in ruins? She didn't have a sense of herself other than as a dead weight, dead weight and patches of darkness. Her thoughts pecked at her: how could she let herself be exposed to this? And then the other thoughts: she had to respond to life, she had to find an answer to her life. Then again: how could she be so mindless, so stupid?

She sat very still in bed and stared at the dark timber on the walls. She tried to breathe with long, slow breaths, tried to breathe herself free from the shapeless burden, the weight of being herself. It wasn't possible to know if she, with her past and her actions, could be accepted among human beings, if she could move among them as if she were one of them.

But even on this morning, she found ways of escaping her anxiety for a little while. They were brief, these moments, small breaks from the ribbon of worry winding through her mind. During these moments, she felt present, almost happy. Then, she almost wanted to head into the dark city and, like an old-fashioned night guard, walk around and light the streetlights one after another.

Her own mother was locked up in that dark city. In there, she was faceless – large and frightening. The darkness had dissolved her features a long time ago; it was too late for Marta to assemble them into a whole again. It was as if her mother's face had been scattered in the dark and the different pieces would never find each other again.

She now longed for that face, longed for it the way you may long for a place, a town, a room. In the short moments when she escaped her anxiety, she felt a deep longing. As a small child she'd never really felt that she'd had her mother, but her mother's face had once been all she'd known. It had been the very firmament of life, and through it, she had come into the world. She'd lived with the scattered and blurred image of that face almost her entire life. Why she'd come to think of it so intensely now, here in Deep Tarn, she didn't know. Something about the landscape had seized her and now it held her. The landscape was breathing, it was a pulse that she could feel, and it was heavy and monotonous and beautiful.

Perhaps the landscape was also a face; perhaps it resembled the first face she'd known. It was a gate, an entrance, to something.

Whenever Marta mumbled something about setting out for Mervas, Arnold and Lilldolly would interrupt her.

"Mervas will be there," they'd say. "No need to be in a rush to Mervas."

They'd show her the way there when it was time, they promised. They'd take a day trip there together in Marta's car since Arnold and Lilldolly no longer owned one, at least not one you could drive. They were content to stay around Deep Tarn now that they were retired and didn't have to chase after money. They had the whole world here, they said. Sun, moon, stars, and forests. Birds, fish, and all the animals. The water and the earth. They had food delivered to them once a month and got their milk, butter, and cheese from their two cows. They grew their own potatoes and got meat from the forest, from their calves and their sheep.

"But Arnold is the one who needs the meat. I'm a peaceful person, I don't eat humans or animals," Lilldolly declared, and emitted her little giggle.

"She's sensitive, that one," Arnold said. "She has looked too deep into the animals' eyes, so to speak. Saw herself in there."

She was an extraordinary person, Lilldolly. And she looked like a little girl, but with wrinkles. Her eyes were small and brown, with a razor-sharp gaze. Her movements were also like those of a girl, light and bouncy. She was like a squirrel. Next to her, Marta felt old and slow, even though she was many years younger.

Since Marta came to Deep Tarn, it had been windy, and the rain from the north had been cold. All the snow had melted, and there was water everywhere. It was an in-between time, a time for waiting. Everything was waiting for warmer weather to arrive and drive every shoot of grass up from the cold, wet ground, and lure the birch leaves out of their casings.

"All this water will blossom and grow green," Lilldolly said. "When the early summer drinks its fill."

Most of the time, Marta followed Lilldolly at her tasks. Arnold was busy with the firewood. They dug holes and spread manure on the potato field and they took care of the animals. When the sky cleared, they walked together from one farm building to the next, over wet paths in last year's grass, zigzagging between rusty old farm equipment and broken-down cars, troughs, and graying wooden constructions. Everything was sinking into the grass, into the ground, moving down into the underground.

"Soon, the wind will be the only thing left here in Deep Tarn," Lilldolly said. "Nothing but the wind, opening and closing doors and windows. It will be the only thing following the forest paths and visiting the houses. This place will become something else. Everything will change, will go back to what it used to be. Nature, she's strong, my daddy used to say. She can conquer cities. This little place will be nothing but a morsel to her. She'll swallow it whole without even bothering to chew."

Lilldolly's laughter rippled through the woods. It was always there, even when she was quiet. Suddenly, at a turn or behind a corner, it would appear again. Or when you stumbled a little.

Marta walked around breathing in the scents. There was the scent of water, of melted ice, and then the scent of burning wood and the odor of soil and dung and decomposing plants. The *lavvu* smelled of sharp wood smoke; the house had a sweet cottage aroma. Around some of the huts and barns there was a faint aroma of tar in the air and arching over all the other scents was that of forest, of conifers and pine needles, of turpentine and wind filtered through branches. Marta let the scents fill her like wine, like a young and vibrant wine. They made everything around her, the light, the deep yet muted colors, become visible as if they'd been created and shaped by them.

Sometimes when she felt tired, she went to the *lavvu* by herself to rest or to write in her journal. The *lavvu* wasn't a simple traditional one, which was what she'd imagined the first night she heard about it, but a wooden structure without windows or chimney that looked like a little cabin or a fort with a cone-shaped roof. She liked to sit in its dim half-light, smelling the wood smoke and hearing the sounds outside as close as if she were out there. She felt protected inside there, childishly safe. She didn't feel the same anxiety she'd had on the first morning; at any rate it was weaker, sort of diluted. All the roads and paths she walked down with Lilldolly were now being sewn into her life and although these paths might have been made with fast, simple stitches, they attached her to something, they kept her in the world. The fact that Deep Tarn was a place on the edge of things, and that Arnold and Lilldolly were outsiders, seemed significant somehow.

One morning, Marta went with Lilldolly to the tarn the farm had been named after. It looked like a big eye and was situated in the woods not more than a hundred yards from the house. They followed an often-used path along the edge of the water and came to a small cabin at the farthest end of the tarn. Lilldolly explained that she lived there during the summer. Once the goats and the cows had been let out to roam the forest for the summer, she'd stay there, that's what she'd always done. A short distance from the cabin was the summer barn, a shelter with a roof and three rough walls. Lilldolly would milk the animals there, where they could also escape the gnats. Gnats don't like roofs, Lilldolly said. Under a roof, their bites are useless.

Together, Marta and Lilldolly started organizing the cabin for the summer. They swept and scoured the floors, aired out rugs and mattresses, cleaned the chimney, and cleared out the woodstove. They placed bunches of budding blueberry branches in glass jars around the hut. Marta felt light and happy, as if she were a child again, puttering about in her playhouse, making it nice. During some summer vacations, Marta and her sister had stayed on farms and at one of them there'd been a playhouse where they could spend as much time as they wanted. It was as if they'd been given their own kingdom to rule, a kingdom where they were the king and queen and their rules were the only ones that applied.

"By midsummer, lilies of the valley will be blossoming here by the tarn," Lilldolly said when they carried blueberry branches inside the cabin. "Tons of lilies of the valley. Then you have to come and visit and pick some!"

Marta never felt as lightheartedly chatty as Lilldolly. In some way, she was speaking the wrong language, and she felt everything she said sounded artificial and stiff, like a newscaster on television. Arnold and Lilldolly spoke as if they were in love with every word and expression they used; as if they caressed them inside their mouths and shamelessly enjoyed using them.

"My, it's fun to have company," Lilldolly now exclaimed. "Even to haul out the sour dung to the potato field! Now, let's see if we can get the woodstove here going, so we can make some coffee."

She'd already started a fire that was snapping and crackling behind the stove door and the coffeepot jerked suddenly from the heat on the burner.

---

"Yes, out here, we're on our own," she continued contently. "Just you and me."

They were sitting on two small stools by a little table attached to the wall right by the stove. Lilldolly took out a piece of the tart-smelling cheese, a vat of butter, and bread cut into triangles. There were cups in the hut and she'd brought sugar in a little bag. They were quiet for a moment while waiting for the coffee. The low door was open toward the water, and on the other wall, the only window in the hut looked out over the forest. It was too early for mosquitoes, and the only sounds came from the birds outside and the low murmur of the woodstove.

Lilldolly settled her searching, vibrant gaze on Marta, carefully studying her, sort of feeling her way across her face little by little.

"This is a good place to talk," she said. "After all, we haven't told each other very much over these last few days. You don't say much, do you? You keep things close to yourself."

She turned the stool around and dealt with the coffee, pouring it into cups and continuing:

"I can see you've got your own story. It's the story that brought you here, and that will take you up to Mervas. I'm not blind, but I'm not going to question you about it. Anyone has the right to keep as quiet as they like. I'm a curious person, of course, but not so much that you have to tell me. You can keep quiet if you want. If you want to talk about yourself, you're welcome to. But stories have to come on their own accord, they're alive like everything else. If they're going to come out, they'd better come out alive, otherwise there's no point."

Marta felt hard and mute during Lilldolly's speech. When she lifted the coffee cup to her lips, she noticed that her hand was trembling; from the corner of her eye, she saw that Lilldolly had noticed too. She desperately tried to think of something appropriate to say, but there was nothing to say, she found nothing. Somewhere inside her, there was a small rupture, a faint desire to place her life in Lilldolly's hands, to simply let her receive it.

"But if you don't want to talk, perhaps I can tell you something? It's something I've never told anyone before, not in its entirety at least. It's not a secret I want to share with you; it's just that it so rarely happens that someone I can talk to comes here. I really feel the urge to tell you, if you want me to, if you want to hear it."

Marta nodded. Of course she wanted Lilldolly to tell her, she wanted it very much. She couldn't remember the last time anyone told her something important, had it even happened before? Yes, of course it had, but a very long time ago. She now sensed something resembling undernourishment. Her life was arid and gray, lacking in stories, people, and fairy tales. This meager existence had made her thin and weak, sort of translucent.

"Yes, please tell me," she said at last, smiling uncertainly at Lilldolly. "I mean it. Tell me. It doesn't happen often to me either. I mean, I've lived alone most of my life."

Lilldolly chuckled, placed a lump of sugar in her mouth and let it dissolve as she sipped her coffee. After this, she put butter and cheese on the bread and chewed and ate for a while. Outside, an osprey shrieked high in the sky, and Marta sat with her hands in her lap letting the stillness envelop her. She had made the right decision setting out on this journey, she thought. She had not been brought off track.

Humans are so careless. That's the worst thing about them. They're so impatient, so rough. Why are they in such a rush? What drives them? Why are they grabbing things so angrily, always causing harm? They push and pull their poor animals instead of sitting down, listening to them, and talking to them so they can feel at ease. It's as if everyone is walking around with a constant storm inside; there's always a headwind inside them, always pouring rain and hail. They trample gentle flowers, tear up moss from the ground in big chunks. They clear-cut the forests as if there were a war going on and everything had to be obliterated. They are so harsh, everywhere and with everything. Children get slapped and banged around. The very earth itself gets skinned and dismembered as if it were a slaughtered animal, nothing but a dead, numb, lifeless body. All this brutal ravaging has made me afraid for life; it has somehow injured and hurt me deep in my heart, at my core. It's as if everything that's beautiful, wise, and simple has been stepped upon, stomped upon. You know, everything beautiful in the world goes straight to your heart as surely as the birds come flying here in the spring. Beauty is reflected in the heart, it places its reflection in our hearts as true and as real as you see the forest reflected here on the lake. Of course you think I'm being childish. But I'm old too, I've lived a long, long time and have been able to think these things over so many times that I know they're true. I've also experienced how all the mean and ugly things in the world have argued with my heart, pierced it so I've had to defend myself with all my might. Yes, I've learned, I've learned that the only thing worth listening to is the longing, my own longing, my heart, you see. That beautiful call inside me is the only thing worth listening to.

*Lilldolly's a bit weak for the animals, isn't she?* That's what they said when I was a girl and didn't want to come into the woods and watch the reindeer be slaughtered. Or when I ran away at the mere sight of my father returning home from a hunt with quails and rabbits hanging dead from his belt. The rabbits were hung on the wall, their big black eyes staring empty, and their long soft ears now useless. I used to sneak out to them at night and tell them I was sorry they'd been shot and cut open, their bellies filled with prickly spruce needles. I'll help you, I told the rabbits. When I grow up, I'm going to help you, I said, still believing that when a person grows up, they can do whatever they want.

But I did eat the meat after all, it was like that in those days, you ate what was put on the table. Sometimes there wasn't much of anything. No. But that wasn't what I was going to tell you about; this was mostly an introduction of sorts because what I was going to tell you happened when I was a married adult.

You see, Arnold and I, we couldn't have children. It was as if fate had decided we weren't going to have any, we were forced to live without little ones even though we longed deeply for them and sort of had waited for them during the years we'd been together. We were already living here in Deep Tarn, it was where Arnold grew up and his mother was still alive and lived upstairs in her chamber like a spider guarding her web. God Almighty, that woman blathered so much nonsense. She said that Arnold ought to find himself another woman so that there'd be children on the farm. She said worse things too, things that made me say no when she wanted me to bring her food upstairs when her legs were too weak to come downstairs. And let me tell you what I think. I think Arnold's mother was a real witch. She put the evil eye on me because I'd taken her sweet boy away from her. As long as that hag was alive, no children were conceived in Deep Tarn. She lived for a long time too. Goddamned stubborn she was, almost rotted completely before she stopped breathing and died. She rotted both inside and outside, her body and soul. Yes, curse her! But finally, she was dead and then she was buried and after that it didn't take long until I got pregnant. I was right, I said to Arnold. I couldn't help myself, I had to tell him. Now you see that I was right, it was that mother of yours who kept us from having children! Arnold said there was no way of knowing if that's how it was. Children come of their own accord and there's no way we can know what they think, he said, and then we didn't speak about it anymore. She'd been his mother, after all, and he didn't like anyone but himself to be speaking ill of her. She was also dead and gone now, the room where she'd lived was scoured clean and repainted and all her old rags had been burned.

The spring after that old hag died, our little girl was born. We named her Anna-Karin, Arnold and I did, because those were the two most beautiful names we knew and together they became even more beautiful. Every morning when little Anna-Karin woke up and opened her eyes, Arnold would call: *The sun's coming up!* It didn't matter if it was in the dark of winter because she was our sun and we danced around her and she shone and spread her light around us so that . . .

I can barely speak about her. Still. It's as if an entire lifetime isn't enough for me to mourn that girl. No. But now I really have to try to tell the story I was going to tell you. It's about Anna-Karin, everything is about Anna-Karin. If you don't know about Anna-Karin, you simply don't know Arnold or me, that's just the way it is. When we had Anna-Karin with us, we didn't have a lot of money. We didn't have a lot of food either, they'd recently shut down the mine in Mervas and plenty of men were looking for work in the area, fighting for whatever jobs there were. Arnold only had work once or twice a week; in between, he'd mostly be at home making tar or going into the woods to fish or hunt. It wasn't always legal to do that during that time, you know, he took what he could get and what we needed. I preferred when he brought fish home, but times were hard and there was Anna-Karin to think of. I had to take care of the meat from the rabbits and the wood grouses, it was food too, and we needed all the food we could get.

And then. Then came the evening during our second summer with Anna-Karin when Arnold came home carrying a calf on his shoulders like an empty sack. It was a female moose calf, you see, a tiny baby, so young you could almost see the remains of her mother's milk around her mouth. Yes, dear God, what a terrible sight it was; I thought my heart would break. I just took Anna-Karin in my arms and ran straight out to him and screamed: "What have you done, you miserable man? What on earth have you done?" I looked at Arnold and saw that he was scratched and bloody and dirty and then I saw the little calf hanging there lifeless on his shoulder. The pretty little head was crushed to a pulp and I just screamed and Arnold told me to bring the little one inside the house so she wouldn't have to see this. But I felt absolutely crazy from what I'd seen and when he pushed me aside to go down to the meadow with the poor calf, I followed with Anna-Karin crying in my arms and I howled and yelled that he was a beast to have killed a child, he'd killed a nursing baby, and did he know what he'd done, did he truly know what he'd done? Arnold screamed at me again to go inside the house with the little girl and stay away, and if it hadn't been for Anna-Karin he'd probably have hit me. I no longer recognized him, it was as if he'd turned into someone else in the woods and something of that evil streak of his mother had appeared in him. And then it was as if I woke up and became hard and silent inside. I thought I would just walk away with Anna-Karin and never have anything to do with that man ever again. Back in the kitchen, I tried to comfort her and give her some wild strawberries mashed with milk, but she just screamed and screamed as if someone were stabbing her with a knife and after a while I noticed that she had a fever and was sort of touching her ear with her hand.

When Arnold came in a little later he immediately asked about our little girl and I told him she had a fever and seemed to have an earache but that she'd finally fallen asleep. Now I wanted to hear the entire story about why he'd come home from the woods with a battered baby moose because I wanted to know if this was really my husband and the father of my daughter or if something had happened out there in the forest that had taken the other Arnold away from me. He sat down, put his head in his hands, sighed, and let out a moan. "There were no fish in the nets this morning," he said. "Then, I tell you, I didn't see a single sign of an animal in the woods all day. So when that female moose with her calf showed up within range, I just shot at the calf, I didn't have time to think, my gun went off and the calf fell but then it got up and the mother probably thought it was dead because she ran away and the little calf followed because wretched me had wounded it. It ran up on the Great Swan Bog and I followed but I was worked up and shaking after that shot and I fell into a deep hole in the bog and half drowned both the gun and myself. Then I ran like a maniac, chasing that calf, cursing and railing at myself. It took an hour or more before I caught up with it over by the saplings past the tarn; it was on the ground, shivering. It was such a miserable sight I wanted to cry when I saw it, it was so frightened and so small and the blood was running from the wound on its side. You won't understand this but it enraged me and my gun was useless so I grabbed a rock and rushed up and crushed its head. I thought I'd leave it there in the forest and just walk home, but that didn't seem right to either it or us after all that, to not bring it, so I gutted it and brought it home."

Arnold told me all this almost without a breath between the words. And I, I'd been sitting there staring at him the whole time while he was talking and it was as if his face gradually transformed into something ugly and foreign and unapproachable. More and more, he ceased to be my Arnold. Instead, he became something large and terrifying and unfamiliar and I became scared of him, scared of the kitchen where we sat, and scared of the bright, quiet summer night outside. I became scared of life itself, I'll tell you, scared of how it can be and what it can do to you. And this fear was so intense that when I heard Anna-Karin whimpering from the bedroom I couldn't move but sat there as if frozen to the chair and I saw Arnold get up and run over to her. I heard his voice as if there were a great distance separating us and he was yelling that she was having fever cramps, but I couldn't get up, I couldn't move my arms or legs or get my mouth to speak. When Arnold came out with the girl in his arms and I saw how sick she was it was as if a great darkness closed in on me and I couldn't find my way out of it, all I remember is how frightened I was in there. Images flashed through my head. I saw the moose calf and Anna-Karin, razor-sharp images that merged and became one. Anna-Karin with her head crushed, her broken little face belonging to the moose calf body dangling against Arnold's chest. And as you must know, that night when I sat in my darkness on that chair, our little girl died from fever cramps while the ear infection moved inside her brain and extinguished her.

When the taxi arrived to take her to the nurse's station, she was already gray and dead and I don't even remember how they transported the three of us in the taxi, I didn't come out of my darkness and I couldn't say a word until we came into the doctor's room and I looked at Anna-Karin where she lay incomprehensibly stiff and still on the table.

He shot her, I said then. He injured her, I said to the doctor and pointed at Arnold. He had to kill her with a rock.

Everything stopped when Lilldolly finished her story. There was nothing more to follow. But a slight breeze slipped into the cabin, swirled around, and left. It seemed to want to remind them of the shiny new world the sun had painted for them outside. The clear, bright air hovered, trembled. The sky that had hastily been swept clean proudly announced its blue color. In the sharp sunlight, the budding, still-naked branches sparkled with crystal raindrops while the conifers, like cattle, seemed to drink the light in long, deep sips.

Inside the cabin, the two women sat within the silence that arched over them. Marta shivered and felt cold from hearing Lilldolly's story. Her hands were stuck in each other's grasp, tightly clenched, like icy clumps. She had wanted to say something after Lilldolly's long story, but she stumbled on the words, they stuck in her throat. She felt as if she were bursting with things to say, but at the same time she knew her voice wouldn't obey her. Instead, it would turn into rapidly spinning blades that cut everything around her into bits and pieces until nothing but the terrible and unrecognizable remained, nothing but bloody pulp.

A bumblebee awakened by the sun paused and buzzed for a moment outside the open door. Outside, the tarn reflected everything in its gaze:

trees, sky, birds. It was an open eye, and the only thing that would make it blink quickly was the wind. It's always watching, Marta thought, and she felt the burning sensation, the effort it took not to close her eyes, to force her eyes to see.

Marta bent her head and peered up at Lilldolly, but she was in her own world. Her hands were like two small animals curled up on her lap and she looked out the door with calm, heavy eyes. Quickly and clumsily, Marta got up from the table and rushed out of the cabin. When Lilldolly ran after her, she found Marta leaning against a thick willow, vomiting.

"My dear child, what's happening?" Lilldolly asked. She leaned over Marta and touched her neck and hair.

"What's going on? Did you get sick?"

Marta eventually stopped throwing up but started sobbing and weeping instead. Lilldolly fetched some water in an old coffee can and wiped Marta's mouth and face and let her drink from her cupped hand. Marta was on all fours with her hair hanging over her face. She didn't want to look up. It struck her that she wanted to be nothing but an animal from here on; it would be a relief. She wanted her mouth to be a muzzle and she wanted to keep drinking from the cupped hand. She wanted to be an animal and hold her face toward the ground and never again stand upright with her breasts and belly and eyes exposed. Now she wanted her sounds to be loud, deep, and hollow; she wanted every sound that left her mouth to be a roar or a bellow.

"Dear child," Lilldolly mumbled, and stroked Marta's back slowly where she was planted firmly on her hands and knees, shaking with tears. She wouldn't let herself be pushed into a sitting or lying position. Lilldolly stroked her as if she were an old sheep, groaning from contractions.

"You can stay like that if it feels good. I'm not going to force you to move. You just stay there and finish crying."

---

"Oh, oh," Marta moaned after a while, her tears pushing and pulling inside her. "It's not me; it's not me, not me . . ."

"That's right," Lilldolly said, leaning her cheek against Marta's head. "It's not you; of course it's not."

"It's not me," Marta tried again. "I shouldn't be the one crying. You should be crying, not me," she whimpered. "This is about you, Lilldolly."

"It doesn't matter who does the crying, dearie. If it's you or me. It doesn't matter."

"But I don't want to take it away from you, don't want to take anything away from you with my own troubles and stand here and. . . You having to comfort me."

Marta had to force the words out between her sobs. It was as if she were pushing them through a perforated wall, which made them come out in mangled, deformed threads.

"You're the one," she continued without making much sense. "I'm the one who, I mean, you're the one – who should be comforted."

"You cry and I'll tell the story. It's as it should be. The one who tells the story can't cry. The one who tells the story has to find her way past the tears if she's going to get anywhere. You go on crying. You can cry for me."

"Yes, and you, you . . ."

"I've had my share of crying, I've cried enough for you too."

"But I can't, can't . . . I can't tell you, Lilldolly. I have . . . but I can't, can't tell you – "

"No, you do the crying and I'll do the talking. That's how it'll be. Now you're the one crying."

Lilldolly's hands kept working Marta's back and shoulders while she talked, they pinched and kneaded and stroked and pushed and Marta closed her eyes and let it happen. She was an animal now, she could allow herself to be stroked, she was an old, ugly animal who had nothing left of shame or pride to defend. It didn't matter that she was sobbing and drooling, that some vomit was stuck in her hair. She could stay here and be without a soul and let her tears stab her apart.

"Let go of your shoulders now," Lilldolly said. "It feels like you have a sack of taters under your skin. There you go. We agreed that you'd do the crying and I'd do the talking. That's what we said. But I can't help but wonder what kind of journey got started. No, don't answer me, you don't have to say anything, I understand it was something you had to do. You've left everything behind, that's obvious, you've got nothing to return to. God have mercy, what don't we humans have to do to be at peace. I want you to know that it's the greatest and most important thing we have to do in life, to find our peace. To stay at peace with life. That was the agreement, the promise we made when we first came into this life. To honor that promise you're allowed to make whatever journeys and do whatever crazy things you have to do. There's nothing to stop you from that, nothing at all. You're allowed to cry, as much as you need to. You can throw up too, go on, throw up as much as you can."

Lilldolly went on talking while she stroked and kneaded Marta's body. But with an unexpected twist, she suddenly and decisively flipped her over so she wound up sitting on her behind. For an instant they looked at each other, a little surprised. Then Lilldolly grabbed Marta's chin and held her face.

"But you can't hide any longer," she said. "That's cheating."

"And you have to watch," Marta said absently. She wrenched her face loose and began rubbing it with her palms. She looked up, present again, cleared.

"I'm sorry, you have to forgive me. I don't want to be like this. Your story was so . . . intense. I hadn't expected it to be such an important story. Such a dangerous story, dangerous for me. I'll carry it here in my heart, like you said, inside what's beautiful. I'm happy, you see, I'm happy even though it doesn't make sense and I'm sitting here like an idiot, like a . . ."

Lilldolly started laughing her clucking, sparkling laughter, sounding like a lively creek between rocks and suddenly Marta began laughing too; she couldn't help herself. She just flowed along with it, floated on the laughter itself. She was sucked into it and twirled around inside it; it was like dancing, swimming, playing in water. All she needed to do was look at Lilldolly and see how her laughter made her jerk and jump and that same bliss moved through her as well.

"Oh dear," Lilldolly said at last. "Dear, how crazy things can be."

Afternoon had come and the sun penetrated and warmed everything. It moved through the top layer of the soil, into the tree trunks and the timber of the houses. It also penetrated the birds' soft down, the fur of animals, the anthills, and the stones. It penetrated your skin, your eyes, placed its sweet, warm sun muzzle in your hand.

Arnold had spread sheepskins on the ground in front of the house and was resting with his hat over his face when Lilldolly and Marta returned.

"Well now," he said from underneath his hat when he heard them. "I'm getting some company here in the sun. At last."

Then they lay there, the three of them, and let themselves be covered in sun. Marta fell asleep almost immediately and dreamed of the boy. He was calling her as she ran from room to room in a big building looking for him. She had to find him; there was something she had to tell him, something important. Good news. Once, he ran ahead of her in a stairway, he was young and held something in his hand, a piece of fabric. Later, he stood in front of her in a sunny spot in a big hall and he seemed to hover strangely and was trembling somehow and it took a long while before she realized he'd transformed himself into a giant bumblebee.

When she opened her eyes again, Arnold and Lilldolly were drinking coffee on the pelt next to her.

"You fell asleep in the sun," Arnold said. He handed her a knife and a piece of dried meat he'd been carving from.

"Eat!" he told her. "It's salty. Good for you."

She pulled herself up into a sitting position and cut off a small piece of meat.

"You see, we're talking about Mervas," Arnold continued. "We're wondering if we should go on that excursion tomorrow. On the radio, they say the weather's going to be nice now. Lilldolly says it too; summer's here now, she says. So we're considering taking tomorrow off and heading up there."

Marta nodded. She felt confused. Mervas, she thought. Would it become real now? For real? Perhaps she ought to go there alone? She wasn't sure. But if Kosti was there, if she was going to meet Kosti, did she want Arnold and Lilldolly to be there too? No, she wasn't sure.

She nodded again.

"It'll be fun," she said.

Arnold laughed and looked from Marta to Lilldolly and then back at Marta again.

"Well, let me tell you, it's been a while since we went anywhere. There was the dental appointment last winter, of course, a couple of tooth extractions and such. The pharmacy, perhaps the social security office."

"And the grave," Lilldolly added. "We went to the grave."

He seemed taken aback, paused for a moment.

"Yes, the grave. We do have the grave, Lilldolly and I." He inhaled.

"Yes," he said, focusing on Marta. "You see. That's how it is. It was a good thing that you got lost and ended up here. This way we get to go on a little trip before we get stuck to this place like moss on the rocks." He laughed again.

"We can go shopping too," Marta said. "And to the grave, if you want. Now that we're going."

"No, that'll be another day," Lilldolly decided. "Mervas is in the opposite direction altogether. That'll be a whole other trip. No, let's go to Mervas. That'll be something else."

She peered at Arnold.

"Yes," he said. "It's another world. Mervas."

After some discussion, it was settled that Arnold would drive. He was the one who knew the roads the best and was used to being on them, he argued. Lilldolly wanted to sit in peace in the back and have space for her own thoughts and Marta would sit in the passenger seat. She'd have a good view from there and that was important, Arnold reasoned, because she had to learn the way to Mervas. Tasso was also coming along, and he got to sit next to Lilldolly in the back, as he used to. They put sheepskins, food, and the coffeepot in the trunk. Then they took to the road.

Arnold was driving fast, Marta thought, but she didn't say anything to him about it. After Deep Tarn's road, they'd ended up on a narrow gravel road that wound through a steep, undulating forest and small ponds like hollows strewn everywhere in the landscape. The spruce trees were sparsely spread; no shrubs or low trees obscured the view. Here and there, a big boulder covered in gray moss rose from the ground. Small ridges pressed against the ground like the backs of animals. Without warning, the trees came to a halt at a gorge that led straight down to another kind of world. Here, everything seemed small and inviting. You wanted to enter among the trees and walk around in those woods. The ground seemed to be padded; perhaps the *huldra** moved there on her soft, springy paws.

*A huldra is a creature in Scandinavian folklore, a beautiful naked woman with a hollow back and a fox tail who lures men deep into the woods then abandons them to their deaths.

But suddenly, the narrow road ended and Arnold veered right onto a wider gravel road that cut straight through a landscape that was completely different. Vast and endless, it stretched out with its enormous lakes resting in depressions between the mountains. It was mostly woods and no vistas, young trees and old growth, the sun like a golden caress over the carpet of berry shrubs between the trees. Sometimes they came upon clear-cuts, large, empty areas, but these areas were forests too – missing, petrified forests without trees, woods in waiting.

They didn't talk during the trip. It was still early in the day and night hadn't yet wholly left their senses. They sat focused, looking out the windows, and stayed silent while the road crunched beneath them and the landscape rushed past. The road continued straight and wide and they passed yet another big lake. Marta thought there was something odd about these large, desolate bodies of water; there were no houses around them. They just lay there as if undiscovered by man. Nowhere had they seen a single house or farm. Only in one place, in a small clearing by a little lake, was there an abandoned trailer. They traveled through the woodland as if they each had their own small part in it. Mile after mile it belonged to itself; trees and animals and people were nothing but visitors there.

The sky was a blue stream lined with the tops of scraggly fingered firs, floating above the road. Marta looked up, following the stream; it was easier than trying to look into the forest. The trees obscured the view, she thought; they were in the way. It takes time to discover that the forest is a place where the space between things matters more than the trees, that it is a swaying in-between world where light and shadows rule. Someone is playing an instrument in there, sometimes slow and gliding, other times jerky and bouncy, a bow of light and shadow slides across the strings of all the tree trunks and branches and twigs. If you want to see the forest, you have to avoid looking at the trees; you have to learn how to look where there's nothing, to the side. That's when you hear the music.

Marta's internal view was also obscured today; inside her, the trees were also in the way. She saw the calf with its crushed, hanging head and thought about Lilldolly and Arnold, thought about what Lilldolly had said the first night she met them, that with this man she shared neither table nor bed. She was now sharing the place where she slept with Marta. But Arnold and Lilldolly seemed like a couple in any case. They didn't seem to be enemies. It was obvious they liked each other. But still, Lilldolly's story had pushed Marta into a place she couldn't escape; something tugged at her. She was caught up in scattered thoughts about the boy and Anna-Karin and the calf, about Mervas and Kosti. Caught up in sudden fragments of childhood memories that kept appearing – her father's spirit inside her, his constant, commanding presence, the fear of his voice raging through the mail slot. Then, her mother's austere features, immovable and stern, enduring it all. She remembered her own feeling of being on fire and freezing simultaneously, of being completely naked and walking powerless across the floor of the stage, of existing without form. She had to be there, had to be there. Caught up in all this, she desperately tried to see over the edge of her own life. But the blue canal above the road flowed through her like a ribbon of forgetfulness, a blue thoughtlessness, a blue oblivion free of longing. It told her she didn't have the strength to figure out what the chafing images and memories had to do with her. It told her she didn't want to know if they were about her life. Or about herself. She really didn't even want to know that they were now on their way to Mervas; she'd soon be there, very soon she'd actually be there.

They'd just passed another lake and come up on an elevated plateau when Arnold suddenly, in the middle of a steep upward slope, slowed down and almost stopped the car.

"Here's the road up to Mervas," he said. "It's easy to miss. You can barely detect it."

"We're here?" Marta asked, newly awake. "We've arrived?"

"No, we're not there yet, but this is the road. It's about two kilometers, as I recall. A lousy road."

That's when she saw that they were just about to pass an almost illegible sign that leaned toward the low birches behind it. She surmised the name more than read it; the sign was flecked with rust, half-eroded and erased, but it burned inside her like a branding iron. One by one, the letters of this name burned their way inside her and now she held the letter in her hand again where she'd first read it; now she felt the triumph she'd experienced when these same letters had appeared in the right order in the index of the big Nordic atlas in the library.

"I can't do it," she said at once with such determination that Arnold immediately hit the brakes and stopped the car.

"I can't do it, I have to go there by myself," she continued. "I have to do it alone."

Arnold turned and looked at her with his iridescent blue eyes and she thought she'd corrode under his gaze.

"So we'll have our excursion somewhere else today," Lilldolly called quickly from the backseat. "We'll go to Reindeer Head Rapids today!"

"I'm sorry," Marta said.

"You don't have to apologize. I thought you'd have us step out here in the middle of nowhere while you'd go up to Mervas by yourself. All right, let's go to Reindeer Head Rapids. Absolutely. We used to do that all the time in the old days, Lilldolly and I, when our little Opel was still running. Yes, we'd go to Reindeer Head Rapids every spring."

He backed up a little too fast from the road to Mervas and then pressed so hard on the gas that Tasso started barking with excitement.

———

"Hush, silly," Arnold shushed. "You're frightening the girls!" He peered at Marta and smiled a little. "I say, you're a difficult one," he said.

A week later, Marta found herself again in her car before the sign that had once pointed toward the mining community Mervas. Now it pointed mostly toward the low shrubs, down toward the ground.

She'd stepped out of her car and stood there staring. The solitude pressed against her, the silence pounded in her ears. The only sounds beyond her own were the wind and the hum of bird voices. The road to Mervas was very narrow, saplings crowded the edges and soon they'd start growing in the middle of the road. The budding green birch trees arched like a tunnel above her and light glittered through the braided branches.

She took a few loudly crunching steps onto the road and discovered that she was walking on asphalt, on cracked, shrinking asphalt. She shivered as if someone had touched her unexpectedly and could imagine what the road must have looked like once, before the woods started closing in from both sides, before the frost from below could freely gnaw it to pieces and partly swallow it. It had been blank and glossy and wide, with a demanding parade of yellow lines running down the middle, and like a general it had brought people through the desolate forests and wilderness into the new and neatly organized place that Mervas had been.

Now the silence was incomprehensible. Trucks and buses and cars had driven here, clusters of children and teenagers had biked down this road, Vespas and mopeds had sputtered down it. In some strange way, it felt as if all these things were still there, as if they'd been preserved and were still occurring somewhere below everything, hidden. Marta kicked the gravel a little as if to resist the impulse to shout to the past, to call out a sorrowful greeting, a lonely hello. She realized that her present was shared by a past that had, in a sudden gust, breathed on her.

Saturated, she walked back to the car, got behind the wheel, and began driving toward Mervas. Branches scratched the car's paint with sad, faint sounds. She didn't take her eyes off the unreliable road, riddled with potholes and rocks and fallen branches. She was forging a track, and she could feel it within herself. It had always been there, a creek, a flowing body of water inside of her; now it had surfaced.

Something large suddenly appeared in front of the car. Startled, she slammed the brakes before she had time to see what it was. It was a reindeer, nearly white, standing but a yard away from her. For some reason it refused to move; it stood glowering at her for a while and then started an easy trot up the road. Marta had to follow slowly behind.

She thought she'd been driving forever when the dense old-growth forest suddenly cleared around her. The reindeer was still running ahead of the car when she came into a birch forest with a patch of grass in the middle, almost like a rotary. The reindeer went to the right, down a slope. Marta stayed in the intersection, trying to figure out where she'd ended up.

A very sparse pine forest surrounded her and soon she discovered, both straight ahead and to the left, a residential area; except there were no actual houses. The foundations were lined up in neat rows, partly overgrown by moss and berry bushes. Staircases and basement windows were still in place. Since no houses obscured the view, the grid pattern of the streets was visible between the trees. A small flock of reindeer was grazing among the remains of the foundations. The scene was so still, so strange. Marta parked on the nearest street. Then she opened the door, but stayed in the car. This silence, would she ever get used to it? It was so serious, so demanding. Each and every little sound had to be let through it, nothing could escape, and the world seemed as close as skin against skin; everything was laid bare.

Mosquitoes flew inside the car; they had hatched in the recent heat. She shut the door. It felt difficult to step outside; the solitude ached inside her. Sooner or later she'd have to go out. Her fear battled her curiosity; she had to go out. The reindeer probably wouldn't attack her; she'd never heard of that happening. If they weren't afraid of walking around here, she shouldn't be afraid either. There couldn't be any bears around if the reindeer were here. Arnold had talked about bears and blueberries, but he'd never mentioned any reindeer.

She took a deep breath, and then stepped out of the car, closed the door, and turned her back to it. Her heart pounding, she looked out over the abandoned community. It appeared to her as idyllic as the neighborhoods of nicely decorated wood houses common in Swedish small towns. But the place also exuded something else. Like a piece of dynamite ready to explode, something was constantly threatening the village's idyllic sense of sleep and stagnation. She sensed a presence, a very strong presence, palpable like a wall – the sensation of a body, a voice.

She forced herself to start walking. To avoid disturbing the reindeer, she walked straight ahead for a block and then turned onto the first street to the left. After about a hundred yards, she came upon the remains of a big building where surprisingly many of the walls were still intact. A cracked staircase led her down to the basement floor and she stepped through a door hole into the largest room. A great willow tree was in bloom there. The corridor behind the room had door frames that all opened to the woods. All floors and ceilings were gone and the ground inside the building was covered by last year's leaves. On a wall in the corridor, someone had written: *I went to school here from 1946 to 1952.* There was an illegible name underneath, *Astrid* something, and a date from an earlier year. Others had written and scratched things on the walls too, but the text had faded.

She continued her walk up and down the streets. Everywhere were signs of habitation, moss-covered columns stood silent among the fir trees, foundations and collapsed basements, small houses and larger buildings. Right where she'd left the car she found the communal laundry room and its cast-iron washtubs. Here, the roof was intact, but a pile of rocks and mortar had sealed the front door. She stood looking in through a window, an oblong, square opening in the moss. The sun had found the same opening and illuminated the floor and the walls with its warm yellow light, a stream of honey on the gray stone. Shards of mortar and concrete covered the floor, and the cracked walls were covered with mold. But no objects were to be found, not a single thing had been left behind. You could tell that this place, this little town, had been abandoned in a very organized way. Even in its deterioration, the precise, businesslike order that had once ruled here was still very much present. A sort of bottomless rationality, an organized decay, seemed to surround her. All appendages had obviously been cleared away before the houses were disassembled. Windows and doors with frames had been removed; furniture, toys, buckets, and kitchen appliances had been carefully cleared out. Only the foundations that would eventually wither away had been left behind, the remains of stairs, the window frames. Mervas was a skeleton that had been picked clean.

Marta once more arrived at the small intersection and now she decided to take the road that sloped down the hill, the one the white reindeer had walked away on. To the left were the remnants of another large building, otherwise nothing but forest surrounded her, denser and more rugged.

After a sharp turn, the woods cleared somewhat to her right. At the bottom of a steep slope lay a big, still lake surrounded by smaller pools and rocks. The water was green and dim, waiting, watching her; it was still, bottomless, and its clear, wide-open center showed how incredibly deep it was. A high fence, made by thick wires, had been erected along the edge of the slope, but the road continued downward and after yet another turn, the woods opened onto hills and sky.

Bright, magnificent space was all she could see. A broad unbroken expanse of piercing green wound its way toward the mountain ridges. It was like a wide river running through the valley, like shining green water. Stunned, Marta gazed out over the landscape, which seemed to go on for miles inland. Somehow, it was incomprehensible, more at home in dreams than reality. Dancing on the sacred meadows of bliss, she thought, and in her mind's eye, she could picture bears dancing with reindeer. But she understood that the beauty was probably a mirage, the valley was most likely poisoned. This plain was like a discharge of the old mine, which had once flowed out of the bowels of the mountain in a river of slag and toxins.

Something else caught her attention. In the foreground, right where the road ended and the plain started, stood a huge stone monument. It could have been the mining tower, a solitary, heavy concrete creature frozen in silence. She walked down to it. Four solid pillars carried an arched ceiling. It was a sad arch of triumph, a call from the past, a disintegrating, cracked memory of something. When she stepped in between the pillars, she saw two paintings on the inside, pictures of Mervas as it had once been: a picture of the community and its houses; and another of the mining site with the tower soaring in its center. "The Mervas of my childhood as I remember it," someone had written below the picture.

Marta suddenly felt very tired. It was the feeling of not belonging anywhere. A pendulum had started swinging inside her, back and forth, back and forth. Did she really have the right to be here? Shame ran through her body again. How could she have been so stupid to travel all the way to this strange, distant place just because Kosti had mentioned it in a note that wasn't even a real letter? She felt more afraid of Kosti than of anything else in Mervas. He might be standing somewhere, watching her, at this very moment. He'd be shaking his head and thinking: She came. How crazy!

Perhaps he was here with someone. It could be a woman. His woman. Now he was going to her, to tell her that the loony woman Marta, whom he'd been with for a few years in his youth, was here. She'd followed him all the way here.

However, he had written "your Kosti" in the letter. How did he dare? Was he trying to make fun of her? Marta stepped away from the monument. The ground was covered with sharp stones and iron scraps. The wind from the plains was picking up and it was dry and cold. She shivered. *What are you doing here?* she imagined Kosti saying. He sounded annoyed, accusatory. *What are you doing here?*

She walked up the long slope again, back to the village. The atmosphere was a little gentler up there, the sun was warm between the trees and the grid of the narrow streets gave her a feeling of comfort. It made her feel that the world was an organized place after all, at least if she behaved herself and remained in the background. Kosti must have come in a car just as she did, but there was no other car here. Besides, it had been six months since he had written her; it was highly unlikely he was still here.

She took one more turn around the foundations before she sat down on the schoolhouse stairs with her sandwich and the thermos of coffee, which Lilldolly had prepared. She couldn't see the reindeer any longer; now she was all alone. The birds were still there of course; amid the chirping she could distinguish the chaffinch's particular string of sounds. She was actually free to go, she thought. Whenever she wanted, she could get in the car and drive back to Arnold and Lilldolly's. She could leave here at any time, nothing was forcing her to stay in Mervas, she didn't have to stay. She hadn't traveled here to see Kosti. She'd come to face herself.

She had the right to be in Mervas. The place was singing around her; it resounded with song. All of Mervas surrounded her like an unusual, gently sung song emanating from between the withered stones and the light filtered through the trees. Maybe she wouldn't be afraid here. Some people can be connected to a place, a certain place, the kind of place that gives itself to you and allows you to hear its song. Marta thought she heard something peculiarly familiar in that song; she recognized it as if it were her own life singing her story, her own voice crawling out from everything that had been left behind and forgotten. It wasn't that she belonged here; she'd never felt she belonged anywhere. But there was a trace of something, a kind of recognition. Perhaps the traces of things are what's most real, the fragments of something, the scent. You can't get any closer to what's real; if you do, it dissolves.

It was at that very moment, right when she was thinking this, when she bent forward to pour more coffee from the thermos, that she saw something on the ground. It was a pipe cleaner, brown from tobacco juice and bent in the middle. It lay next to the base of the stairs and beside it was a small pile of ashes and half-burnt tobacco. She lifted the pipe cleaner, smelled it, examined it with her fingers. Her hand was trembling. Kosti, she thought, and the notion was somehow inconceivable. He was here. There was no way this thing could have been here since the previous winter.

"You should spend the night here! Why would you want to stay overnight in Mervas? No, you go up there and have a look and then you'll come back to Deep Tarn. You can do whatever you want, of course, just know that you can come back anytime. I'll say, you are being secretive. Incredibly secretive. When you return you'll have to tell us. Something. You have to promise to tell us something."

The words had streamed from Lilldolly's mouth in the morning when she was making sandwiches for Marta. It was now evening. A blackbird was lecturing from the top of a fir tree behind the school. The air had cooled; there was an icy edge to it, something cold and hard left behind from winter. The blackbird was speaking to Marta with Lilldolly's voice. In the evening, when all other birds have gone silent, the blackbird speaks in a particularly serious tone. *Come back*, it said. *You should come back to Deep Tarn. Don't stay there in Mervas*, Lilldolly urged, in the slow, deep voice of the blackbird.

The evening breeze swept some leaves from one place to another on the gravel in front of Marta. The branches of the blooming sallow in the school's largest room stirred in the wind. She sat on the stairs struggling with her doubts, trying to grasp what she wanted. Cold, she buried her hands in her jacket pockets. She had wrapped the pipe cleaner in some toilet paper and put it in the glove compartment before moving the car up to the school building, where she felt most at home.

There was one place in Mervas she'd rather not have known about. She sat pondering it. It was at the far end of the village, and all streets led there. She'd noticed an arched, slanting roof over a door opening. At first, she figured it was an ordinary ground cellar. But then she'd looked through the gaping door frame. A stale wind had hit her face, a strangely strong, cool and damp breeze that seemed to come from below, from the dark depths. She'd seen a long stairway, and something was shimmering down there, probably water. Beyond that, everything was black. But that wind told her something. It was no ground cellar, it was bigger than that, much bigger. Probably a path leading down to the mine.

The fact that she was in a mining town where roads and paths led down and into the mountain felt natural. However, this opening into the dark had filled her with fear and rage. The burning, short-fused anger she felt reminded her of something, reminded her of being forced to obey. Where she now sat curled up on the front stairs of the school, she could clearly recall how the gaping door frame became a mouth breathing its dark, powerful presence into Mervas. The odd feeling seized her that this mouth would suck up everything outside it, that it would pull everything unmoored and movable toward its shapeless internal darkness, would swallow anything light, kind, comforting, and warm. In there, down there, she thought, everything would dissolve; leaves, people, pieces of wood, stones, everything would dissolve into darkness.

She was freezing, and tried to shake off her thoughts. But the mere knowledge of that opening with its stairs leading down to the shiny water made her shiver with discomfort and also robbed her of the feeling of freedom that was so precious to her. The feeling that she was free to leave whenever she wanted to, that nothing forced her to stay in Mervas.

*No, nothing is up to you*, the chasm hissed.

She was meant to be forced, such were the rules of her life no matter how much she tried to resist.

She tried to listen only to the blackbird, who was still singing, tried to stay with the warm, low voice chanting such wise and simple things, balanced things, about life. It had found a place beyond everything, where there were no demands. A song without rage. He was free.

The blackbird sings the Song of Songs, Marta told herself. The blackbird's song is great, she tried thinking; the greatest thing is love – and the song of the blackbird.

But other voices insistently crowded in on her and said other things, the wrong things. She felt their hard grasp burn around her wrist, felt the strength of that grasp, how she'd been dragged around, forced.

She had initially planned to explore a bit during the rest of the evening. From studying the map, she knew there was a small lake right behind the school, a little ways through the woods. At the lake, she would find a hut, the map said. But she'd become too scared now. Obstacles had been raised inside her, she had to stay on the school stairs tonight, and she couldn't leave. She could sleep in the car later, the tent seemed unpleasantly thin-walled. If she slept in the car she could also easily escape if she had to.

A black circle on the ground in front of the stairs showed where people had lit bonfires. Marta pushed her anxiety aside and gathered a sizable pile of dry branches, leaves, and some birch bark. Then she started a fire. The sun was low in the sky and it slowly rolled north from the west. In a few more hours, it would momentarily dip below the horizon. The sky would never get completely dark, the sun would never sink that low.

When the fire crackled and burned, she felt calmer. Suddenly, she understood why humans had once needed to master fire. It was when they'd been driven from the Garden of Eden, when they were alone with themselves and the immensity of the world. With the help of fire, exiled and abandoned ones sought to protect themselves from the gnawing and ultimately crushing fear. The god of fire now protected her too; she and the fire had a pact against what lurked underground.

She took a piece of smoked whitefish from the lunch box and began eating it with her fingers. Carefully, she removed the thick skin and pinched the tender fillets lightly and gently so they came off the bone. Her fingers dripped with fat, and the aroma from the fish, heavy as it was, made her feel full. *Imagine that, I'm here*, she thought, and briefly felt elated. *I'm sitting here by a small fire in the vast sea of trees, I made it out of my apartment, yes, I broke free and came all the way here.*

Someone else now lived in the gray rooms where she'd been shut in for so many years. Those rooms didn't exist any longer, the rooms where she'd lived alone, and with the boy. They were now repainted, refurnished, all traces of her were gone, all traces of the boy, and the traces of her own catastrophic reaction on the day he turned fourteen.

Embers pulsed faintly among the last logs on the fire and the sun disappeared behind the treetops in the north. Marta forced herself to stop ruminating and spread a thick sleeping pad in the back of the car. She arranged her things so that only the driver's seat was empty and accessible. She really wanted to wash the strong smell of whitefish from her hands, but it would have to wait until morning. Then, she'd go down to the little lake and greet the day by the water. If she'd had a little more foresight, she would've gotten some curtains for the car before she left. Now she had to sleep in the light and hope that she'd made the right calculations so that in the morning the car would be in the shade, away from the sun.

A flock of geese floated across the tin-colored sky. Night had fallen on Mervas and the surface of the lake rested without a ripple. Supernaturally green, the white night light that seemed to come from nowhere rose from the plains behind the mine. Around it the mountains lay sphinxlike, guardian animals in the silence.

Marta fell asleep as soon as she lay down inside the car. The visions that had filled her head and danced behind her eyes as soon as she closed them swelled and grew like sails filled with wind. They carried her into a dream where the images melded and separated and transformed while she moved deeper into the sometimes familiar, other times foreign dreamscape.

The morning had come creeping into what was actually still night-time. A couple of mosquitoes had entered through the small crack of the window that she had left open and they now clung to the walls, gorged with her blood. She opened her eyes. The light was mild, fuzzily gray, and she had time to think that it would probably be an overcast day when she spotted the man who stood looking at her a little ways from the car.

He was large and bearded, and his hair was speckled with gray. He was wearing a shapeless green jacket and had a slight stoop. Marta didn't get scared when she saw him. She knew it was Kosti and it was somehow very natural that he was out there. His gaze was completely focused, and he kept looking into the car as if his eyes were searching for something to hold on to in her features. She felt his gaze fumble over her, searching.

Perhaps he didn't recognize her. Maybe he couldn't see her real face. It was hidden beneath a thick skin of years, settled behind a mask of tired middle age. She now saw that he was crying. It hurt him to see her, hurt him to see what life can do, how harsh it can be. He stood so heavy and stooped out there in the gray light, and she saw his tears running down his cheeks and into his beard. He'd also gotten old. His face was grooved and darker than she remembered. It was more rugged, burdened; all of his quick and sensitive boyishness was gone. She wanted to cry like him, let the tears flow. But she just lay still watching him. Neither of them moved. Something had happened to time itself; they had both stepped out of it and stood to the side, watching. They calmly looked at each other, looked through all the years gone by, everything that had been their lives. It was like a photograph in developing fluid slowly taking shape out of white nothingness. Shadows and lines appeared, darker, sharper. Each waited for the other, called soundlessly to the other.

She sat up at the same moment he took a step forward, and gasped for breath. His face was so deeply and wrenchingly known and beloved; now, at this distance, she suddenly felt how much it had always been part of her life, how close it had always been, how frighteningly close. She untangled her legs from the sleeping bag and unlocked the door. She was trembling all over when she opened the door; her hand trembled, her arms and her legs trembled. She stood in front of him, he was still staring at her, and they took each other's hands and then held each other hard, very hard.

With her mouth against his shoulder, she said:

"You wrote to me. Why?"

"Sometimes it feels like we're getting old. I've thought about you, Mart. These last few years. I didn't want to die without seeing you again."

She opened her eyes. The sun was bright outside but Kosti wasn't there. She was still bundled up in the car. Before her thoughts caught up with her, sleep pulled her into its arms again and she continued dreaming about Kosti. She was on a train and stepped off at a small, rural train station, one of those stations in the middle of nowhere under an open sky. Kosti stood at a distance. He raised his hand and waved to her. This time, he was beardless and his hair wasn't gray. He now looked like the Kosti she had carried with her throughout her life. They weren't in Mervas either, but on some big country estate in Russia. All around them, the freshly plowed earth shone brown, and the fields were endless.

III

June 17

I awoke from my dreams covered in sweat. The air inside the car was humid and dense, as if I were inside a big mouth, inside my own mouth, and I was inhaling the air I had just exhaled. Even so, I remained still. I didn't crack the window. The best thing was to just lie still. I felt ashamed of my dreams, my head full of Kosti. I also had a vague and simultaneously persistent feeling of insecurity and infinity. I didn't know for certain what I'd experienced during the night, wasn't sure what had happened and what hadn't. I felt pulled back and forth between dream and reality, and as the boundaries of the two worlds blurred, I couldn't determine where one ended and the other began. The bearded man with gray-speckled hair who'd watched me at dawn, was he part of the dream? I lay remembering the way he'd gazed at me, and something wasn't right, something about him ran against what I'd seen in my dreams; it was as if he were made of a different matter, rough and resistant. Perhaps it had been a dream, but I'd seen him stand there crying; he'd appeared grave, yet his presence had been almost ridiculously real.

Maybe I had actually seen him; it wasn't impossible. For a fraction of a second, in a moment of clarity, I could've seen him, only to tumble back into my uneasy dreams again, holding him in my arms, the image of him in my embrace. I must have dreamt the rest; that I stepped out of the car and we held each other, held everything that would never come true. I was hopelessly stupid, blinded by delusion. Oh, why do I always have to be ashamed of myself? I had the unpleasant feeling that Kosti knew the rest of my dream, that he stood hidden from view and laughed at me, laughed at my image of us together, holding each other close.

My hands still smelled of smoked whitefish. An intense smell when you've just woken up, greasy and intimate. My feelings crawled through me like insects or crustaceans. My hands had an obscene smell, as if I'd done something during the night I shouldn't have done. I tried to tell myself I had to get up and go to the lake and wash; I'd looked forward to greeting the morning down by the water. But the night weighed heavy on me. I couldn't push it away. Instead, I had to follow the crooked paths toward it again, return to the dream images and the mirages. Everything had to be clear and certain inside me, those crustaceans had to stop crawling through me before I could get up. Without deluding myself, I also wanted to be able to feel that I'd come to Mervas for my own sake, and not to see Kosti.

I hadn't dreamt only about Kosti during the night, I'd had other dreams too. One of them was about the boy, a nightmare. I recognized it; I'd had it before. It was one of those nightmares with different variations on the same theme. The most common dream was about animals, various animals that I'd neglected, that I'd forgotten to take care of.

This one had been about the boy. I'd completely forgotten that he existed and suddenly I realized with painful clarity that he was inside the decrepit shed outside and that no one had been in there for months. I knew I had to hurry, that I had to go out there at once, but different things kept interceding. People showed up, I had to go away on trips, and time kept passing while my awareness of his being out there became more and more impossible to endure. Finally, I stood before the crooked door where tall, sharp-toothed nettles grew. I had to take a big step over the nettles to push the door open. It was dark inside. The small aperture barely let in any light. The dirt floor was black and cold, and I knew it was a death room. The boy was tucked inside an old wood trunk attached to the wall, and it was utterly incomprehensible that I'd let myself forget about him. The last time I'd been there, I'd made the bed nicely and fed him. The room had been entirely different then. The whole winter had gone by and I hadn't even thought about him, about his existence.

The lid of the trunk was open and I leaned into its darkness. There was still something inside it, I could see that. But if it was still the boy, he had become incredibly small, almost like a bird. He showed vague signs of life, a scent, a breath. He seemed to be disintegrating, and I didn't dare touch him. I couldn't; everything was revolting and disgusting. I didn't understand how I could do this to him and felt afraid of what people would say if they knew. The only thing I knew was that I quickly had to find him some milk, that I had to feed him milk through a small tube.

When I came home again to fetch the milk, and perhaps a medicine dropper if I could find one, things, people, events blocked my way, and after a while, I'd forgotten what I was supposed to do. A long time passed and when I once again remembered the boy in the old trunk out there, all I wanted to do was press my hands against my eyes and ears and not know about it, I didn't want to be part of it any longer. Shameful notions of "removing him" from there, of getting rid of him, burned through me, licked at me like tongues of fire.

As if walking against a hard headwind, I made my way to the shed, which was now even more decrepit. Part of the roof had collapsed, and daylight fell through the hole like through a large, ragged wound. The trunk was closed. I opened it slowly and immediately noticed something among the rags on the bottom, but this time it was barely moving.

June 18

I am always walking in my own shadow. My shadow falls on everything I see and everything I touch. My shadow is heavy with my presence, the way a rain cloud is heavy with water. I don't understand how other people do it, how they manage to be human.

Yesterday it started raining, and that was just as well. I couldn't do anything but stay on the sleeping pad in the car and stare out the window while the drops beat against the roof and my thoughts dug their paths and tunnels through me. I'm walking around with a longing in a constant state of alert, an impatient, chafing state of waiting. It is a longing for love and I don't know what it wants with me, I don't see how it could be useful. It is digging a hole through me, digging a hole to give my emptiness room to grow. I know my life cannot be shared by anyone; to burden another person with my issues would double the guilt and pain for me. If I can't even be close to myself, how could anyone else? And still, this voice inside me is alive, this ripping longing for love so strong I'm beginning to think it's bigger than me, bigger than my own life.

Today I emerged from my torpor and went outside. In the morning, I followed a path leading to the village. The path opened onto a small beach, which was clearly man-made with its gravel, sand, and pebbles. The natural shores around the lake consisted of bogs and impenetrable swampy areas. The lake was small, perhaps a hundred yards wide. But there's something about water that makes you feel good just by looking at it. When I stepped out on the little beach and stood there looking at the surface, I suddenly felt moved. It is difficult for me to describe why, but small lakes like this one in the middle of the woods, they lie there like a caress, a soft caress. There's something open and forgiving about them; they possess a quiet healing quality.

The surface of the water was so still that the cloudy sky was reflected in it. It was as if the lake were calling me. Come inside, it said. Let me surround you. I took off my boots and my pants and took a few steps out into the water. It was icy cold; nevertheless I stood still in it and let the cold push and pull at my feet and shins. I rinsed my hands and wet my face, then I quickly ran out of the water and pulled off the rest of my clothes. Naked, I stepped into the water again and it was as if I were meeting someone in it, as if I were seeing a lover. The water had awakened a desire in me; I washed my armpits, my crotch, I rinsed my face again and again, pulling my wet fingers through my hair: I pulled and pulled so it felt like dull plow blades against my scalp. The water was so cold it hurt, but I had been seized by a thirst for it, I couldn't get enough of it; the cold, soft water would make me come alive. It would awaken me, rinse the dirt off me. I would emerge hard and clean, shining like a pebble by the edge of the water. I stood there scooping up the water, splashing it over me, thinking that water really was the origin of life, everything was made from it, and I wanted every pore in my skin to drink and be full.

When I finally got out, both my arms and legs were numb from the cold and my fingers ached. But the depths of me felt remarkably warm, delighted in being alive. Something had begun stirring inside me, a desire to be part of the world.

But the euphoria I had felt by the lake in the morning quickly dissipated. I guess I can't handle that much happiness. Little by little, the day filled me with gloom; darkness arose in me like an endless, gray December dusk. I walked around aimlessly searching for the cabin. It hadn't been visible from the lake as I'd expected, but I knew it had to be somewhere close to the water west of the beach where I'd been.

In the birch forest I had seen when I came to Mervas were plenty of paths leading here and there, a tangle of tracks among the rubble and the ruins. This was where the outdoor dance floor had been; the little kiosk was still standing, its windows broken, garbage visible inside. Fifty years ago, Lilldolly had danced here with Arnold and the men from the bachelors' barracks; it wasn't difficult to see where the stage and the dance floor had been. It was as if the forest wanted to hold on to the memory; grass grew here, budding buttercups and red campion.

One of the small paths by the dance floor led into the woods and I soon ended up in a dense forest of young pines. In an instant, mosquitoes surrounded me like a wall; suddenly they were everywhere with their thin whirring sound and feathery touch. They danced around me and attacked me at the same time; their bites burned everywhere, on my neck, my scalp, my hands, throat, and face. I was seized by a deep, claustrophobic fear and walked faster until I was running, surrounded by a buzzing cloud. The cabin appeared before me without warning. A rough gray wooden wall materialized between the tree trunks. I stopped and heard my own breathing along with the whirring of mosquitoes while I angrily swung a leafy branch around me.

---

Here was the cabin. I gazed at the back of it; the trees were close together in front of the windowless wall. The fear the swarm of mosquitoes had produced in me grew larger, rose to the surface, and at once everything seemed ominous: the forest, the dull gray wall of the cabin, the notion that someone could be inside it. I turned around and, like a hunted animal, ran back through the woods.

Mervas in June

Marta, Mart!

This isn't the first time I have sat down to write to you. But all the
other letters I've either thrown away or burned. Some I've placed among
my journal notes like memory plaques. The letters often got incredibly
long; if I'd saved them all they'd be an entire autobiography. I guess I've
tried to understand my life by writing about it, to understand and explain.
As you can see, I've failed. That's why I decided that this time my letter
to you would be concise. It would still be a real letter, not just a note
like the one I sent you last fall (and assume you received). My cowardly
notion was that if you wanted to see me, you'd sooner or later show up
in Mervas. If you do come, it will most certainly be in the summer, and
then this letter would be here, waiting for you.

I'm a coward. I don't know if I want to see you. I really don't understand why I'm writing to you at all. Something in me has pushed me to
do it, and I finally decided to go ahead.

Enough rambling. This was supposed to be a concise letter.

For many years, I've lived periodically in Zimbabwe, participating in
the excavations of the old gold mines there. Seven or eight years ago,
when I happened to be home for a while, I saw a story in the newspaper.

It was a brief notice about a mother who had killed her severely disabled child. She'd been evaluated for mental illness, it said, and had been in such a state of shock she had to be hospitalized.

I knew immediately. I knew it was you, Mart. My body knew it, my muscles, my nerves, and my cells. I began shaking violently where I sat; it was as if an electric current were going straight through me. My tea spilled onto the newspaper. I screamed, just screamed without words. I felt so terribly sorry for you. But it wasn't just that; without quite understanding it at first, I also felt responsible. I knew I was involved and responsible. I was part of this story. What I'd read in the newspaper was part of my own story, part of my own life. Isn't that right, Mart? Isn't it?

With time, I've understood that my actions also were part of this story, that they were part of it in a way that couldn't be changed or erased. It was as if I had in some impossible way been with you. As if I had been present. It all flashed in front of me as in a dream sequence, a nightmare; everything that had happened was replayed in my mind over and over.

You might think that I'm barging into something I ought to stay away from, something that concerns only you and that no one else has the right to talk about or touch. But what I want you to know is that you weren't alone when it happened. What we'd had together and what I did to you was part of why you did it.

It isn't always simple to know what's important or crucial in your life. I think it's possible to miss it altogether. That's probably the easiest way. When I came back from the Orkney Islands and heard that you'd had a child with another man, I thought all ties between us were cut. I wanted it to be that way. I wanted to be free from you. You were frightening, disruptive, and I felt swallowed and crushed by you. I thought I could let you disappear from my life. That is, until I read that notice in the paper. It hit me – all this time, I hadn't really been part of my own life. I had escaped into something else, changed my name, assumed another fate.

But I never contacted you. I resisted the urge. I thought it would've been foolish, that my inclinations were sick. When you received my little note, I'd already written impossibly long letters that I'd thrown away.

I'm still not sure. I still don't know why I'm writing to you. Perhaps I'm not writing to you as much as I'm writing to the part of my past tied to you.

I've been allowed to use this cabin, where my letter will be waiting for you, until the moose hunt starts on the first Monday in September. Mervas is an odd place, odder even than it may first seem. I'm down in the mine most of the time. I've found something down there that I can't write about, an entire world.

You're welcome to stay in the cabin so you don't have to camp. I would like you to stay in it.

If you want to come down into the mine (and to everything else down here), the easiest way is through the tunnel that opens onto the village. It looks like an ordinary ground cellar. The other entrances have more or less collapsed or are underwater.

I'm a coward. Please forgive me.

Your Kosti

June 20

Slept in the cabin. Had a terrible night. I lay in the lower berth of the bunk staring at the grainy, thin twilight inside the cabin. The light was a shivering gray specter whose warm, enveloping darkness had been taken away from it. My thoughts moved around in the room like anxious shadow animals, sniffing and listening. I almost thought I could see them flickering over the walls. Herds of fear ran down the slopes as if they were being hunted, being egged on by the thoughts and visions spinning in my head. The terror seemed to hatch in new places all the time, one vision after another appearing in long, painful sequences. And I had to keep looking at them; I couldn't avert my eyes.

I've secretly longed for Kosti the way someone may long for the warmth of a nice bonfire. But the pleasant and warming fire turned out to be a dry roaring pyre, the kind of blaze that can set the very air on fire with its electrically charged flames. The fire I had sought out suddenly wasn't tame at all, it was reaching for me with glowing arms, wanted to pull me into it, wanted to consume me. Standing there, unscathed and cool, Kosti smiled sweetly while trying to pull me into the flames.

"Do you want me to tell you about The Day?" he asked with a whisper, his voice so eerily intimate that it made me hate him.

That's when I saw the cabin walls contract and expand around me like the inside of a mouth. I had to breathe or else I would suffocate. A loud moaning woke me – it was coming from my own mouth. I leapt out of bed, flung the door open, and ran outside.

The sky was vast above me. I took a deep breath. Exhaled. A streak of silky, thin gray fog covered the blue and in the northeast the sun was pumping its sheen through the thin layers of clouds. The light seemed so pale and mild and birdsong was everywhere like thousands of tiny stitches of invisible patterns.

I drank some water from the bucket by the door and then sat down on the stairs feeling at once heavy and relieved. Perhaps things weren't so bad, I thought. It's all inside me already, it is not even sleeping. Deep down in that dark city, no one dares to sleep. The vigil goes on there day and night, guarded behind glass and minutes, in seconds and in years. It's all inside me, I thought. And actually, everything is already afterward, it has already happened.

It's odd, but just then the final scene in *Uncle Vanya* came back to me. It was a TV version of the play that was aired when I was young; I think I saw it a couple of times. Lena Granhagen played Sonja and Toivo Pawlo the uncle. In the final scene they sit by their desks with big ledgers open. It's quiet and almost unnaturally still in the room; only the rasping of their pens can be heard. All the ruined love and rebellion, the dreams that blossomed and withered, the burning humiliation and almost annihilating disappointment – all this was contained in the scene but as if under a lid, perhaps like a seed, a small capsule – completely saturated with what has been and is now over. It's like an exhalation, a long, blubbering exhalation. It is the very image of *afterward*.

In actuality, I've probably always carried that scene with me, I've heard that kind of silence and seen them in front of me, how they sit there sighing, dipping the tips of their pens into the ink, their hopeless calculations. It's so painful, yet there is also a sense of relief in the pain. The sense that it's now over. It's over and at the same time, it will continue. Neatly, it will be noted down under the right heading, be over and continue for all time.

As I write this now, I think of Lilldolly and what she said about finding peace. That the greatest, most important thing we have to do is to stay at peace with life.

I can't write anything about Kosti's letter. I can't see my own thoughts through the muck and sediment that have been stirred up.

June 23

The day before yesterday, I had to go shopping. My provisions were getting low and I longed for fresh things, for produce, bread, and milk. It became an excursion, a jaunt to a foreign galaxy. The closest store is in Storsel, about twenty miles away, beyond many winding gravel roads.

But there's actually no way to leave Mervas. Or, it shouldn't be possible, shouldn't be so easy. All I had to do was get in the car and drive away. It didn't seem fair. It was like cheating on an exam. The whole deal, the entire agreement seemed rigged. To remain loyal, which is what I want, I can't diverge from the path, can't turn my gaze away. I have to keep looking. That's the first commandment of my childhood: you have to keep watching. It's strange that a child can understand such things. But I just knew that not to look was to abandon something. And I think that's how I have to respond to my life now too, by not diverging an inch from the solemn and serious situation I'm facing. That's exactly how I have to respond. It's not about penance or mortification, but about honesty. Because I don't want to abandon myself.

Yesterday it was the equinox. I ate some pickled herring and new potatoes that I'd bought. For dessert, I had Belgian strawberries that were so shiny and deep red, so large and well shaped, I almost doubted they were

153

real. Later in the evening, I took a walk on the wide-open plain below the mining shaft. That place doesn't seem quite real either. A poisoned, emerald-green fairy-tale landscape, a big, hyperrealistic painting to enter. But in some way, I'm still attracted to it, as to some lovely pasture, the dream of a better life. Then, I would graze there, be a grazing animal on the green earth, on the vast river of flowing green grass.

But once I was out there, I felt a little scared. The wind howled so forlornly, and I could see it moving through the rough, sparse grass like a wind spirit, a strange creature without a body, out hunting. For some reason, I feel less frightened if I can walk along water, so I started following a creek with copper-colored, dead shores that ran along the other side of the gorge. Thick copper sludge rolled up against the water's edge and the water itself, which looked brownish red, also seemed unnaturally clear. It signaled danger; I didn't even want to dip my fingers in it.

The world is empty, I thought as I walked along. Just that: the world is empty. Here, on these flayed, meat-colored shores, it becomes visible; here it becomes true. The world is empty. The words ran through me repeatedly, although I didn't quite understand them. I didn't even agree; a few yards from the creek, the bare soil turned into sparse, sheared grassland. I saw tiny birch saplings fighting for survival; no taller than the blueberry shrubs, they stood there sort of burnt, tormented, trying to grow. The world isn't empty at all, I wanted to think, and it's populated by life and rage. But I couldn't snap out of the feeling of meaninglessness. It really wasn't a judgment about the world as much as a sudden and very clear experience of it. A sensation that it's empty and incomprehensible. It was exactly as I had once learned in school: light doesn't exist by itself but only through the reflection of everything else. Some thoughts are puzzling. Sometimes they fall on you with a kind of clarity that disarms all your objections. The world is empty and incomprehensible, yet we still have to believe in it.

The sun was still high in the sky even though it was late and the light, twinkling so brightly in all the greenery and glittering in the water next to me, it made me squint. Around me, the forest undulated on its mountains like a ship at sea, light green where there were birches, dark green where there were pines, and nearly black where spruce grew. The ground crunched lightly beneath me, it was flat and even, easy to walk on, and I felt like walking all the way to where the plain and the valley ended.

I had walked for maybe a mile or so when I saw a moose calf. It shone. It stood completely still on the other side of the creek, watching me. It was as if a secret heat radiated from it, a pulsating, vibrating heat rising from its fur. I too stood completely still, watching the shining creature, the long slender legs, the body they carried, and I was filled, filled with what I saw. The calf's gaze seemed to move inside me and took me out of every familiar context into what is new and foreign. It was such a strong sensation of presence, of intense and strange presence, that I suddenly saw myself as someone I'm not. I was imprisoned in it, contained by it. It filled me with a peculiar joy. I can't describe everything that twirled up inside me, but there were so many images; the moose calf hanging across Arnold's shoulders, little Anna-Karin, who was now dancing here, and the calf, who wasn't dead but trembled with life. It had returned and the boy would return, everything would come back to life here, in this brief passing moment, but that was enough, it was enough.

"The heart doesn't have a mouth that can speak," I suddenly heard my sister say.

"Yes, it does," I said. "A different kind of mouth. When you're speaking with God, you only speak with your heart."

I wanted her to understand. It was of utmost importance that she understood. Because it wasn't about my believing in God. God existed. Children only know what adults believe. Of course, I was no longer a child, and now, I knew nothing. The calf turned around in a flash and was gone without a sound.

Afterward, I knew I'd been touched, that something had happened. I started walking back with quick, light steps; my body felt electric, I floated across the ground, I ran upstream along the creek. My sense of time had vanished, my feeling of exhaustion was gone. I was soon sitting on the steps in front of the cabin with a small fire crackling in front of me. It was night; the light was soft and blurred. Kosti's letter lay next to me, I had reread it now and his voice had reached me, I had allowed it. I could feel his presence, his eyes on me, his fingertips over my skin, his words marching through the streets of my city.

That's how it has to be, I thought. You have to be forced out of yourself. You have to let it happen.

June 24

I see it as if through the opposite end of a pair of binoculars.

It's me.

It's me with my arms tightly crossed across my chest.

My hands closed around my shoulders.

My upper body rocking, rocking.

It's me, rocking and rocking.

The police entered the apartment. My big, heavy child was lying dead in his own blood among the broken chairs, the potting soil, the shards of glass and china, the plant parts, the cake remains, the spilled soda. That's how I sat, I'd been sitting like that for an eternity already, that's how I had to stay, I turned to stone sitting like that.

It's not I who remembers. It is my body. How I was in the hospital later, horrified, horrified. They tried to straighten me out, sometimes by force, sometimes with medications. But my body was a muscle that had twisted itself around my core of horror, my fingers dug into my shoulders as if they wanted to take root there and grow into my skin. The aides cut my nails short and bandaged my hands, but the wounds on my shoulders wouldn't heal; in a frenzy, my fingers dug deeper into the ulcerated, aching flesh. Hungrily, they ate their way deeper into the pain, I wanted the pain, I wanted to reach it, I wanted to reach it more and more because I had nothing else.

I know that I was limp and barely conscious for long stretches of time because of the medications. But that clutch lived inside me like a memory; I used all my energy trying to reestablish the hold on my shoulder, I fumbled for it from deep inside my blurred state; nothing else was clear to me except that and the rocking, the rocking of my upper body back and forth, being part of a rhythm, a rocking hold, as if something held me, as if I were part of an order.

Sometimes I could hear a thin whine coming from my lips and it frightened me as if an alien lived inside me. I emitted no other sounds. I was mute. I was mute for a long time, months, a year, I don't know, I've never wanted to know much about this. I was in my own world and there was no time in my world, there was no beginning and no end. I was in my place, imprisoned and unreachable, I was inside the boy's voice, I was filled by it, I was the voice box for his voice to rage through. I was spared the images, I couldn't see them, they were twisted, dissolved, hacked into something so awful and despicable I could not look at it. But I could hear, and my whole being absorbed sounds and echoes. I heard the boy's voice, sequence after sequence, I was spit-roasted over his voice as if over a flame, was lowered into it as though into a scalding bath. I heard the boy as he sounded on The Day and I heard him as he sounded when he was newborn and wouldn't stop crying. I knew I had to sit with my arm muscles tense and tightly crossed over my chest and my hands gripping my shoulders. I had to keep rocking and rocking; it was the only way I could maintain myself.

They couldn't understand this at the hospital. There, they thought that it was the rocking alone and my stubborn grip that was the source of my insanity, and they put a lot of effort into making me stop. They didn't understand that, to the contrary, it was the only way I could protect myself from insanity. It was my defense. When they used force trying to straighten me out and even tied my hands, one to each bedpost, I was obliged to defend myself as if they were trying to drown or strangle me. I wrangled and spat and kicked and wriggled, not to fight with the staff but to protect myself from the voice inside, to get rid of the boy's voice inside me, because it was tearing me to pieces. His voice told me what I was.

There was no way out for me. I was mute. No conversations could save me from my entrapment. The medications they gave me made my horror blurry and dim and made me lose the crucial strength in my arms and legs, made me twitch and shiver uncontrollably. What finally happened, what after a very long time gave me the courage to stop defending myself, was a miracle.

One day, a new aide came to my ward. He came into the room where I sat curled up around myself, rocking. It was late morning and my breakfast tray was still on the table by the window, I suppose he came in to fetch it. He stood there just inside the door and looked at me for a while and I noticed him too, I saw that it was a new face and that he looked so young he was almost still a boy. He also had curly black hair and brown eyes, so just a glimpse of him stirred something inside me. That's what my boy might have looked like if everything hadn't happened as it had. Yes, it could have been my boy standing there looking at me, it could have been he.

That's when the miracle occurred.

He came up to me and put his face close to mine. "Come on, Mommy, let's go for a walk, you and I," he said.

Mommy, he said. He'd called me Mommy and the word cut into me like a scalpel, like a razor blade, it cut through all the walls and defenses, straight through me, and everything stopped and for an instant I stopped rocking and sat completely still staring at him.

It was like a sudden thaw, I think, what then happened in me. As when, on a chilly February day, the sun suddenly makes the ice melt from the rafters, and the titmouse starts to chirp. It happens only for a moment, a brief moment in the afternoon, then the cold will once more turn the water into ice. Everything takes a long time, I didn't immediately release my grasp and I didn't stop rocking and I didn't start speaking, but I'd experienced that sudden thaw, I had paused for a moment and seen that aide, that boy, I'd glimpsed his face and brought it into my world. Slowly, for days and months, he made porous the stone I'd become, so wind could blow inside me, water could trickle through, and he finally made me step out of my own frozen grasp, as if out of a building, and take a few steps across the floor. When he came to see me every day, he simply inserted his arm into my hard-pressed elbow and he whispered: *Come on, Mommy, let's go for a stroll.* And we did.

June 26

The days pass so slowly here I sometimes don't know what to do with them. The days went by slowly at home too, but it was simpler there, I was sunk into a kind of meaninglessness in which I wasn't expecting anything in particular, not from myself and not from life itself. I was in the apartment most of the time, walked around among the tracks and traces, through my dark, unlit city. I felt no real responsibility for how my days passed and what I did with them. My life was unmoored and I guess I thought I just had to accept that.

When I was about to be released from the mental institution, the counselor told me I ought to get a new apartment and move to another part of the city. She said I ought to start a new life and get away from the place where everything would remind me of what had happened, everything that bore witness and whispered of the past. There were neighbors who knew too, she hinted, neighbors with knowing glances I would have to greet on the stairs.

I've killed my own life, I'd wanted to say to the counselor, but in reality I just nodded to ward her off.

If I'd been able to speak then, if I'd had the words, I would've said that I'd killed my life and there is no new life, no other life, waiting for me.

All I have are the traces and ruins from the past and that's where I'll be. That the neighbors know what I've done is nothing compared with the fact that I myself know.

When I returned to my life in what we call the real world, it was actually comforting that the neighbors knew. That they'd seen the rotating blue lights of the police cars and the ambulances, that they'd read about it in the paper. They also knew that I too had been a mother, they'd seen the boy with me, they'd witnessed our life together and held doors open, occasionally helped me carry things. What was hidden in the way they looked at me didn't scare me much. The things hidden inside me were what frightened me most, my own story and everything lurking in the darkness where you couldn't see anything, the hole where my story had been lost.

I've been thinking about *Uncle Vanya* again. About when everyone had left, when they were alone, Sonja and the uncle, when they sat there, afterward. That's when they saw their lives again; they saw themselves and everything around them, the farm that needed to be cared for, the muddy road, and the light filtering through the treetops. Perhaps it was fall, I don't remember when it was in the play, but let's say that now, a flock of ravens lifted from the largest tree, everything was real in that inescapable and meticulous way, it couldn't have been any other way. And they saw that this was their life. They saw that was where they were, that they existed. They bent down over it, they crouched over it, got hold of it; let the tips of their pens labor and scratch it down. Without even thinking the thought, they knew that's how it was, how it had to be. And I know it too. Kosti's note told me. I exist. This is my life that I'm living, letter after letter.

It's been hot today. The heat here is unusual, a dry, pine-scented inland heat, a strangely stifling forest heat. Hardly a breeze in the air, just the bright light from straight above, the heat trembling in the reflections of the sun. There's an alarming number of mosquitoes around and today the horseflies arrived too, everything is coming alive; I can feel it, in the midst of the silence and the solitude there is a sense of rush, of urgency.

I woke up far too early this morning and couldn't go back to sleep even though fatigue ached in my eyes. When my thoughts had cast me from one side of the bed to the other for nearly an hour, I still couldn't sleep, so I got up. Outside, the sun was light yellow and already warm; I brought out my sleeping bag and sat inside it, leaning against the wall where the sun hit. Between the trees, a stone's throw away, I could see the surface of the tarn; its colors were still deep and warm. Each morning, the world is new and untouched once more; it comforts me, the mornings are never old and worn. I sat there thinking of Kosti, wondering what he was doing down in the mine, what it was that he'd found down there. I also wondered when he was planning to come out again. Because I'm here waiting, all the time. At any moment, he could be here in front of me. At night, the sounds always come together to seem like *his* steps through the woods, *his* movements getting closer. Sometimes I imagine that he's sneaking around the cabin and peeking in through the window and the cracks in the wall; I can almost hear his breathing and the sound of his hands against the plank wall.

But the sun shone on my face and it was bright and I closed my eyes and let it penetrate my skin to warm and thaw me. Behind my closed eyes, blacks and reds were dancing and I let the sun melt down my thoughts and heat them up until they simmered and became fluid, and like liquid copper could reach everywhere, into the narrowest pathways. I thought about my mother, I reached for her; it was her face I wanted to touch. But my older sister kept coming between us, obscuring my view. She stood there protecting Mom's body, she blocked the entire image of her and I wanted to tear her out of the way. But everything was as if submerged in water and my sister slid away from me with the image of my mother like a shadow behind her.

I saw myself too, saw myself constantly heading straight into my father's voice: the rumble, the barrage of gunfire, the heavy, lethal detonations. I'd been sent there because that's where I was supposed to be, running along the front lines like open prey. Again, I tried to get rid of my sister, pry her out of the picture. We were in the kitchen now, in our first apartment. I pushed her as hard as I could, and she fell to the floor and began crying. But when I then looked at Mom, she had my sister's face and with this mask over her real face she yelled at me and pushed me out of the kitchen and into the dark, scary hallway where Daddy came home at night and where the cleaning cupboard was and the carpet beater and the gloomy coats on their hangers. I now stood in the hallway of my childhood and it grew and grew; the coats hanging in it became a forest of dim green fir trees, the tall, bone-white closet doors became house walls in a big, insulated neighborhood of high-rises. Under my feet, the brown-speckled linoleum floor was about to collapse and open into a hole. Far, far away, I saw a door open; a rectangle of light fell across the floor and I tried to call out, tried to scream something, anything.

I woke up soaked in sweat. For a long while, I sat pinned to the dream images floating around in me. Then I remembered something from my childhood, an event I'd never thought of or remembered before.

This also happened in that first apartment we lived in. I couldn't have been very old. I was in the bedroom and Dad sat on the edge of the bed with my older sister across his lap and he hit her bare bottom. Mom was in the kitchen, pacing back and forth. My sister wailed and Dad poured his enraged litanies over her as he hit. I stood in the doorway watching. Suddenly, I ran up to Daddy and started jumping up and down like crazy, yelling: Hit me too! Hit me too! You have to hit me too! You have to hit me too!

I then remember how Mom came rushing into the room and grabbed my ear and dragged me out of there.

"You ought to be ashamed!" she growled at me.

And I still curled up in shame when I thought about it. Beneath the deepest level of humiliation there is something else altogether that you're searching for, that you need to live, yes, even to survive.

June 28

I know there is violence inside me. It is hidden in there, under my skin, behind the bone of my skull, in my nerves, in all the arteries of my body; it is the swelling, slippery muscle of violence itself, a secret animal inside me.

Violence is inside me, naked and shiny, I can feel it, I have it in me, I've inherited it and it has survived and been reincarnated and when it awakens in me I rear up on my hind legs and beat the air with my hooves. I've entered into violence as if it were an ancient tongue, an old dialect that speaks to me and overtakes me. There is a passion inherent in the violence, a longing to be obliterated by it, a desire to become even more violated by giving in to it.

I'm not trying to excuse myself. I'm not defending myself and I'm not saying that the violence inside me is incurable, congenital, a handicap. All I want is to see, to see down into that dark kingdom where so much of my life has taken place. The film from the day of the boy's death is down there too. It is still undeveloped and very sensitive; it cannot stand any kind of light. I know that the images have to be bathed first, and I think that's what happening with me right now. The images are being bathed in my darkness in order to learn how to endure light. It's odd. Before, I didn't think a human life could be so rich. That it could contain so many layers. Now I feel a kind of softness inside, I want to bend, bow down to it.

Everything I've written here in Mervas ought to have begun with the words: Kosti isn't here yet. But I don't want the days here to be about Kosti, about his absence. They are about me. They are about what's present. This morning I found his car. It was hidden on a small street behind the water-filled mining holes; I don't understand how I could've missed going there, I've wandered through every corner of Mervas. It was a dark brown Fiat. Locked, of course. In the backseat was an old blanket and I suddenly got it into my head that I'd seen it before. Suddenly, I began to cry. "You're feeling sorry for yourself," spat a contemptuous voice inside me. And I agreed, I thought I was pathetic. But I still had to cry. I cried because there were no kind hands to hold my shoulders, no one I could lean my head against. I cried because the memories burned inside me, made me contract.

I've stood at the top of the stairs that lead underground several times, but I haven't been able to make myself walk all the way down; my legs have gone weak each time.

Sometimes I wonder if the lilies of the valley have already faded in Deep Tarn. Lilldolly and I would walk around together picking big bouquets of them. There are no lilies of the valley here. I often think about the little girl they lost, about Lilldolly and Arnold, their world, into which I had been welcomed.

On the days before the boy's operation, he had to be scrubbed clean each night with a special disinfectant soap solution. I was so afraid that he'd die during the operation; they were going inside his head after all, to cut him there. When I washed him with the strong-smelling soap, I thought that it was like a ritual cleansing before a sacrificial slaughter. The animal that was to be sacrificed had to be very clean and prepared before it was handed over to the sacrificial priests. The soap smelled of incorruptible ritual and was so alien on the small, soft baby body in my hands, so foreign to the boy's own scent. Now I was following directives while I prepared to give him away. After doing this, I would, for better or worse, place his life in the hands of strangers who spoke a different language, a language that came from the outside instead of from the inside.

The operation did go well in the sense that he survived and stopped crying and twitching. But at the same time, it was as if they'd cut him off from himself, as if a connection had been severed. His spirit couldn't find a place to rest in his body afterward, he had no way of expressing himself, there was no city that was his own city, not even the city of tears was left. But what I kept thinking of was those cleanings, that particular kind of cleansing, the preparation.

June 30

For once to wash yourself clean. I don't know. Perhaps it's not dirt that I want to wash off. But rather a sense of presence, of myself; an invasive feeling. A consciousness that never gives way, that isn't about anything in particular but simply about being, about existing. It's a feeling so intense and infringing it's like being slowly grated into shreds, like being scraped against sharp holes, no part of me is spared, no surface left alone.

I'm supposed to be alive; I've understood as much. I have to keep living. All the deeds evident on my body, like fingerprints all over me, like dirty, inappropriate hands, Daddy's hands, mostly Daddy's hands in addition to my own, they will remain. I was Daddy's girl. I was the apple of his eye and even though he beat and humiliated me as much as the rest of the family, I was somehow his, part of his sphere. My mom was inaccessible; she sat with my older sister and the younger siblings and I stood outside their sphere and looked at them as if they sat in a spotlight of some kind. I longed for my mom – or perhaps I should say that I longed for Mom since she wasn't mine at all. At any rate, I stood outside and longed to be with them, with Daddy's hands, his presence clinging to my entire body like a virus.

I think it was because I was standing there to the side that it became my responsibility always to watch, that I was the one who had to witness everything, not just how Mom was humiliated, or my siblings, or myself. I had to watch Daddy too, and not walk away when he gave in to his fury. Sometimes I think my sister is the kind of person who spared herself, and I can hate her for that. She protected herself from seeing and didn't participate or feel guilty; she just sat there with Mom like some noble victim. I was already tainted from the start, my heart couldn't release me from getting mixed up and dissolved and touched and I often think that this was my fate, exactly this. It was meant for me. I don't claim that I'm any better than my sister as I write this, I just envy her. I will never be clean.

Inside me, the boy's gaze and spirit and what I've done are preserved. It is now part of my life. You can't run away from your deeds; they become hands on your body and you have to live with them, force yourself to remain human with a voice and a face. I knew this afterward, when I was rocking and mute. I was in the kitchen with the boy where he lay on the floor wailing in despair, I was there constantly and would never get out.

I'd made him a birthday cake, a lovely birthday cake. We admired it for a long time together before I cut into it. Then I had to witness how he couldn't eat it. I fed him spoon after spoon, but the cake kept falling out of his mouth and down his chin and chest. I couldn't stand it. I just couldn't stand it. At first, I was overcome with sorrow. I couldn't bear seeing that he couldn't live. And those eyes of his. Trapped inside of him. In those eyes I glimpsed his own terrible sorrow of not being able to do anything. Of being so helpless. Something in me snapped. Rage welled up. A rage that told me to defend him, in some way defend him against all the frustration and impossibility he was experiencing. I began beating him, beating his body and everything that hindered him. I began beating the obstacles out of him that cut him off from life, beating the curse out of him that he'd inherited from me, everything but his gaze and his longing. I beat him. I wanted to break something inside me. I thrashed out with anything I could reach, chairs, bottles, I flung anything I could get hold of, flowerpots, plates, cups, spoons. I threw them at him. At the one I saw. At myself. At the world. At his inability to live. At myself. I was responsible. I had given birth to his misery. At the same time, I screamed. *No!* I shrieked. *No, no, no!* I screamed in a terrible voice.

It was when it was already too late and he'd fallen from his wheelchair and lay in a mess on the floor that I saw him looking at me – how his gaze burned, concise, relentless. That's when I came to my senses. He wasn't me, his eyes said, he was separate, his fate was his own. A wide gash in his head was bleeding and suddenly the whole apartment filled with his scream and I fell to the floor and slid my hands under his head and placed my cheek against his and I whispered *I'm sorry, I'm sorry*, but not a sound came from my lips and I could feel life leaving him, could feel how it stole away from him and was gone. I carefully removed my hands and sat up and prayed to the God that couldn't possibly exist, prayed to him to let me die with the boy, to let it all end. I've broken the fundament of life, I've broken the covenant, so let me now die with the boy.

I'd cut him off, cut off his gaze upon the world, killed his gaze. Sebastian's gaze. And his eyes weren't mine, no, not even his pain or his disappointment was mine. There's space between people, and it is necessary, it's a boundary that must not be crossed, you have to stay behind it. *There's space between people, and it is necessary, it's a boundary that must not be crossed, you have to stay behind it.*

I must not say the words: I killed my boy whose name was Sebastian, I crushed his head the way Arnold crushed the head of the moose calf. Those words are unspeakable. How could I have told Lilldolly? Yet she's the only one I've met whom I'd even considered telling.

"Be calm, my child," begins a poem by –

---

IV

It was evening, already late, when Kosti arrived. Marta was sitting at the table writing in her diary and he just stood there, in the doorway.

"Sorry for barging in," he said, and his voice sounded large and deep in her ears.

She inhaled.

"I didn't hear you. I didn't hear you coming."

Then they didn't say a word.

"Shall we . . . Shall we say hello?" Kosti asked.

Marta closed the diary and placed her palms on the tabletop to pull herself up. Inside, she was tumbling round and round.

"Are you in pain?" he asked.

"No, no, I was just surprised to see you, my legs . . . I see that it's you, I recognize you . . ."

Suddenly, she felt his hands around her waist; he had helped her up, he held her, and she remembered what it was like to be touched, how incredible it felt. They now stood face-to-face, very close; she looked at his neck, the skin had become thin and wrinkled.

"Of course you recognized me," he said amiably. "I recognized you too."

"Yes, but that's not what I meant. I recognized you from seeing you here in Mervas. You stood looking at me early one morning when I lay sleeping in the car."

He didn't respond and when she looked up at his face she thought he looked distressed.

"So you saw me even though you were asleep?" he asked, almost teasing.

Marta said nothing. She recognized him now, the way he was, the way he behaved.

"Shouldn't we say hello?" Kosti said again. "I'll start. Hi, Mart! Welcome to Mervas!"

"Hi, Kosti," she whispered.

And they embraced, but not as hard and long as in her dream that first night, but more tentatively, anxiously; they didn't quite know how to connect. Perhaps they were also embarrassed by all the years that had passed by and made them old. By everything they didn't know about each other. They remained standing for a while with their hands hanging. Kosti stepped aside and took off his rubber boots and hung his green jacket on a crooked stick driven into the wall. Marta removed her diary from the table and tucked it into her bag under the bed.

"Have you seen *Uncle Vanya?*" she asked Kosti. "The version they showed on television a long time ago . . ."

"Ah, you mean the one with that actress Lena Granhagen, and whoever else was in it . . . No, I didn't. You used to talk about it back then too. About that performance."

He watched Marta, sort of surprised, and laughed.

"Well, I've been thinking about it," she said in a slightly stiff monotone. "Don't you think that all that's happening now, that it's a kind of *afterward?* As if everything has already happened. That our meeting here is – a kind of *afterward.* In some way. I can't explain it; you have to have seen the scene I'm thinking about."

"But I don't think that everything has already happened," Kosti said. "I don't even like that notion."

"Are you married?"

He shook his head.

"Have you been married?"

He shook his head again.

"Why not?" she continued. "Why have you never married? Then you have no children either?"

Her voice, which had become hard and shrill, suddenly broke.

"Why the hell didn't you get married and have children?" she sobbed. "Then it's all nonsense! Then everything is completely meaningless!"

She tried to get past Kosti and get out of the cabin, but he blocked her way and caught her.

"What are you doing, Mart? Stay here, come on, look at me."

His grip was fierce, she thought. He was stronger than she was. But she looked down and averted her face, it was contorted with tears that would not spill and she didn't want him to see it.

"I've got to get out," she whimpered, and tried to wriggle loose.

"Pull yourself together. You can at least look at me!"

She turned her face toward his but kept her gaze down.

"It's too much. All this is too much."

He moved his head so he could meet her eyes from below.

"Yes, it is, and that's exactly why we have to talk and look at each other," he said. "Not throw words around as if we were splashing water and then running away. Right?"

She took a deep breath and looked at him. "I guess you're right," she said quietly. "But I'm not used to it . . ."

He laughed.

"No, it's not easy for me either, to see you after almost twenty-five years. I mean, it's not easy for either of us."

The grasp around her upper arms had loosened, but she couldn't see anything, there was a storm in the darkness, a storm raging through the dark city, she could hear its sounds: sheet metal, glass, wind through the shaft.

"Are you hungry?" she asked with a great distance in her voice, as if she were someone else.

"Yes, finally! Yes, I'll take out something for us to eat. Let's set the table and make it nice here. I've got a bottle somewhere too. For God's sake, Marta, calm down a little, will you? We're not strangers. We've come here to see each other wholly of our own free will. Why don't we try to be a little happy, a little lighthearted?"

She looked at him, at his face, which made her feel at home. A deep feeling inside, she thought, and now she was smiling too, she noticed how the smile tore at her face, how it was pulling it to pieces. She lifted her hand and carefully stroked his cheek.

"You've grown a beard," she said.

"Yes, that's what happens when you don't shave."

He let his fingers lightly brush against her face.

"And you have wrinkles," he smiled. "Tiny, fine wrinkles."

It felt as if the touch gave her a face, as if he were drawing it with his fingertips.

"I found your pipe cleaner," she heard herself say. "Over by the school. I've got it in the glove compartment. That's when I knew you were here; it was before I found the cabin."

"And my letter? You haven't thanked me for the letter!"

"Yes, it made me happy. But these things are difficult. Difficult for me. You know, I've been so lonely. I don't know exactly what life has done to me."

"But I told you that you weren't all alone."

"Yes. But perhaps that's not how it is."

"If it hadn't been true, I'd never have contacted you."

"I'm sorry. I don't want to hurt you."

"Now, Mart, now we're going to set the table and make everything pleasant. Let's try to be *here* for a while, *here!* Everything isn't in the past, even though much is. Can you agree with me about that?"

She looked at him. Oh, this was Kosti; this was how he was, now she remembered.

"Let me smell you," she whispered. "I want to feel your scent."

He put his arms around her and she pressed her head against his chest and neck and inhaled that nice, grassy smell of his, mixed with whiffs of his pipe tobacco and mosquito repellant. Her eyes burned and then the tears came like a river. She didn't sob, didn't make any crying noises, the tears just fell.

"I'm not sad," she whispered. "I don't want you to think that I'm sad."

"No, I know that," he said. "I've cried too."

"I know," she said. "I saw you crying."

"Yes, you saw it when you were asleep, didn't you?"

He let his lips touch her eyes, first one, and then the other. She saw that he smiled a little.

Marta's voice, whispering out of the half darkness.

"Kosti, Kosti, are you awake? Can I tell you one more thing? About afterward. I want you to understand what I mean by afterward. It's what comes afterward, after the tears and the screams, after the great infatuation and after the crazy dreams that haunt you. It's when you make a cup of tea and you know it's over and you sit at the kitchen table dipping the tea bag in and out of your cup, and the apartment is completely silent, there's only the light of your lamp and silence and the steam from the tea on your face. It's afterward, you see, after all your losing battles – and the terrible shame that's left – the shame of being who you are. It's after all that, after the tears, when you feel your body soften and give in and a stillness comes over you. You're sort of a small child and your mother has finally heard you, heard you crying and fussing and screaming and now she has lifted you up and is holding you tightly to her. Yes, you know what I mean, it's afterward and a sense of calm, a heavy, warm calm spreads through you – "

Kosti turns in the bunk above her. "But what you're talking about is death – "

"No, it's not about death at all. I'm talking about consolation. About atonement. The consolation afterward."

"I think I understand, Mart. But I have to sleep now. I'm already almost asleep. But can I also say one more thing, before I fall asleep? It's strange that it doesn't feel strange when we touch each other."

"Yes, it is strange. Good night."

"Good night, my dear, my own dear – "

After a moment's silence, Kosti's voice comes from the upper bunk.

"Mart? Are you sleeping? Have you fallen asleep?"

"No, I'm awake. Barely awake."

"Can I tell you something else? One more thing. I want you to understand what I said, what I wrote. It's important, you see. It's important that you understand. You weren't alone, Mart. I was part of it, part of what happened. Even though you feel all alone, even if you felt alone then, I want you at least to try to accept what I'm saying because it was a big thing for me when I understood that. It was incredible. It shook me; my entire life was turned upside down by it. But I knew that I was responsible for what happened, knew that my life also was determined by it, that my fate belonged with yours. I'm not saying that I've suffered like you or that I've experienced the torment you have. I don't want to take anything away from you. I only want you to understand that you weren't entirely alone, not entirely – Can you understand that, Mart? I've got to get an answer from you because sometimes I've thought that I was simply crazy, just out of my mind."

"Kosti? Kosti. It's not so easy. It feels like I'm about to break; I understand what you're saying, I'll try to absorb it. But I have to do it little by little, I can't take it all in at once. Your solitude becomes enmeshed with you. It sticks to you, covers you like skin. But I'm happy. You hear me? I'm happy that you're here."

"I'm happy too. Let's say good night now. Let's sleep."

"Good night. Sleep well."

out of the ashes

I can see through the darkness now. What was blurry is clear. Now I see so clearly in the light of the extinguished lamps. I see her, the woman who was my mother. Now she will be sacrificed. We children are sitting on the floor, completely silent. All we have to do is watch. It's Daddy, he's on top of her pushing, and he's pushing life and death into her womb. It's as if the lights had not been extinguished but lit. A light beyond words falls on them. Someone has to be sacrificed. Someone always has to be sacrificed in order for the others to see. And darkness settles. That's also how it is. Darkness settles.

In the morning, Marta woke up before Kosti. She was afraid. Without making a sound, she took her clothes and slipped out of the cabin. She dressed outside and drank some water from the bucket. Then, with fear somersaulting inside her, she started walking. She didn't know where she was going; she walked where her legs carried her.

Down on the slope, the mining tower looked like a big animal, a solid, immobile body drinking its own shadow in the early morning light. She walked in under the structure, between the four heavy legs and under the concrete belly, which had cracked in an intricate pattern of tangled tendrils. She curled up there, on the ground, and tried to breathe. It was as if someone or something had chased her out of her sleep and away from the cabin, along the path and down the hill. She was dizzy. She wanted to hide, but how was she to know what a good hiding place would be when she didn't know what was pursuing her? Were the woods a good hiding place, or the branches of a tall tree, or the narrow beach? Was the mining tower a good place?

She grabbed tiny concrete shards and sharp gravel from the ground and squeezed her fists tightly around them. It hurt; it was meant to hurt. She pressed the sharp shards against her face. They cut into her skin. She moved her hand around and around against her cheek. Then she began crying. The tears stung on her face and she pushed her forehead as hard as she could against the rough ground. Her whimpering turned into small cries. She was afraid of Kosti. She knew that now.

She struggled to her feet and tasted blood. Together with the tears and dirt, blood ran down her face. Shards and small pieces of gravel stuck in her skin, as if she were a stone wall. The mining tower wasn't a good hiding place, Kosti could easily find her there. She had to keep walking, had to move on until there were no paths or roads to follow. Fear fluttered inside her like a flame in a strong draft. She didn't understand why, but she kept thinking that Kosti was an evil force, that he was dangerous to her.

She walked into the woods and the mosquitoes descended on her in huge, hungry swarms. For a while, she tried to ignore them, but it didn't work. Another, older fear seized her; she was squeezed between the two kinds of fear, paralyzed. Now she was the prey. She sank onto the mossy ground, hiding her face in her folded arms. The mosquitoes bit her where they could, her neck and scalp, her hands. They bit through her clothes; they were everywhere. She lay there trying to endure it, but suddenly she couldn't take it anymore. Her scream was so loud it astounded her. Then her crying grew quiet and miserable; she was a lump on the ground, her back was shaking.

It didn't take Kosti more than five minutes to find her. He had been standing by the mining tower, looking out over the vast plains below, when he'd heard the scream. It was a terrible scream. He wasn't certain that it was human, that it was Marta. But he immediately started running toward it, shaken and frightened. He skirted the edge of the forest; stumbled over branches, fell to the ground, got back on his feet. When he saw Marta, he froze. She heard him and turned toward him. Her eyes shimmered strangely green in her bloodied, soiled face.

"Marta! Mart! What happened?"

She pulled away from him when he got close, and rasped something he couldn't hear.

"Was it an animal?" he asked, but she shook her head.

She felt so tired she thought she'd never be able to move again. Kosti studied her face carefully.

"You did this to yourself," he said harshly. "You hurt yourself, you idiot."

"I fell," she whispered.

"Don't even try. I'm not stupid. You did it yourself. Come on, we have to get back home before the damned mosquitoes eat you alive."

Marta made herself heavy; she wanted to be a boulder, impossible to move.

"Come on now," Kosti repeated, and tried to catch one of her arms, or a hand.

"You did it," she said. "*It was you.*"

He stepped away from her quickly, as if he'd scorched himself on her. He slid his hand across his face, looking at her without speaking. She sat staring ahead at nothing. The only sound between them was the floating, unpleasant hum of the mosquitoes.

"Perhaps we shouldn't have met again," he said finally, as if speaking to himself. "Maybe it was all a mistake. Perhaps we should part from each other again. That might be best for both of us."

A whimper from Marta silenced him. She was crying. He hesitated briefly, and then barked at her.

"Say you're sorry or I won't touch you. I won't help you!"

She twitched at the tone of his voice, and from the corner of her eye, she saw that he'd gotten up and was getting ready to leave.

"I'm sorry," she cried. "I'm sorry. Of course it wasn't you."

She felt him come close and embrace her; his arms surrounded her like a nest. Carefully, she began rocking in his arms, he didn't try to stop her, he moved with her, cradled her. When after a while she turned up her face to look at him, his eyes were red and filled with tears.

"This isn't easy," he murmured. "But now we really have to go home and take care of your face. There are tiny shards everywhere in those cuts. Foolish woman! I hope you have tweezers with you, because I don't."

"I think I have some in my toiletry bag."

"Good girl. Come on, let's go."

He held her up as they walked. As soon as they got out on the road, the cloud of mosquitoes was dissolved by the wind.

"I feel like saying something mean," he said after they had walked for a while.

"Go ahead."

"I was just thinking that when we return to the cabin, it will really be *afterward* for you. Then we're going to truly confront what comes *afterward*."

She tried to smile, but her face was stiff and hurt so much that it turned into a grimace instead.

"You're not being nice," she said.

"Neither are you."

It was a lovely evening with warm, sweet-smelling air, and the sun's golden light shimmered over the forest. The blackbird was singing, but Kosti and Marta stayed inside. She was stretched out on the bottom bunk with a wet cloth on her forehead, listening to Kosti. He sat at the table with the pipe in his mouth and a cup in front of him. With her eyes closed, she was listening to his voice, to the nuances of his tone.

"So you could actually say that it's there, in Zimbabwe, that I've lived my life. The periods that I've been back in Sweden have mostly been like stopovers. I've come home to prepare for the next trip, or I've been back to arrange things so I could stay away longer. I don't know why, that's just how it turned out. Perhaps because I never got married and started a family."

"And there was no woman in the picture?"

"Yes, there was someone. For almost ten years. She was Danish. Worked down there as well. An archaeologist. Well, that's another story, I'll have to tell you about Gina some other time. What I want to tell you about happened long after she and I parted. It was three, four years ago. I was at an excavation in an area south of Bulawayo, by the Matobo Hills, not far from Bambata, you know, the cave dwelling. It was me and another Swedish archaeologist. He was from around here. His name was Gustav, Gustav Jonsson. He was several years older than

I. We lived together for almost six months in one of those bungalows left over from colonial times, a wonderful stone house with a dining room, a library, and a couple of studies and bedrooms. It was very British and very elegant. But the house was completely isolated, a couple of miles from the nearest village and hours from the closest city. So we spent a lot of time together, Gustav Jonsson and I, long workdays of digging at the excavation site, ten miles from the house, long dark evenings and nights in the house. After dinner, we often sat talking on the porch, in the dark. I really appreciated that I'd had the good fortune of sharing living quarters with an older colleague this time. Mostly I work with people in their twenties and early thirties. Nothing wrong with that, but I think I needed the stability of being around someone older. I was sort of lost, lost in my own issues. I didn't feel wise or experienced at all. Just to hear someone say: 'Well, when I was your age . . .' I really needed that."

He interrupted himself and glanced at Marta.

"Are you listening? Or have you fallen asleep? I can't see your face under that cloth."

"I'm awake. I'm listening."

"Anyway. One night Gustav and I stayed up late, sharing a bottle of brandy. He began telling stories from up north, where he grew up. He told me about an old shut-down mine in the middle of the woods, in the middle of the wilderness, and about a small mining town that had emptied when the mining ceased. There wasn't a single house left there now, and no people. Just some concrete blocks, a valley contaminated by copper, and the remnants of a stone wall. He told me there'd been countless stories about this mine when he was growing up. It was still active back then and there were stories about the place that were older than the actual mine."

He was quiet for a moment and fiddled with his pipe, packing the tobacco and trying to light it even though it sizzled and crackled with moisture.

"It was said," he continued, "that deep inside the mountain, underneath the mine, there was a hidden entrance to an underground tunnel. It was allegedly twenty, thirty miles long, possibly even longer. No one knew how old the tunnel was, but there were naturally plenty of stories about how it had been created. It was said that it had been built during the reign of Queen Christina, when they were mining for silver up on Nasa Mountain. That it was the Sámi who had made it in order to save their gods and goddesses, to keep their shamans and their elf drums away from the Swedish authorities. Some people claimed that even though the Sámi had built the tunnel, they hadn't done it on their own; it had been done with the help of magic. More realistically inclined individuals argued that it was a natural tunnel, that an underground river had passed through the mountain a long time ago. According to all the stories, the tunnel was supposed to lead to an incredibly beautiful island. It was surrounded by wide, wild torrents and could only be reached in one way: through this tunnel. It was said that on this island, gods and goddesses still wandered around, and there was a herd of shining white reindeer. Hundreds of elf drums were also hidden on the island, but the shamans that had escaped with them had obviously been dead for a long time. Well . . . as you may understand, Mart, it was an incredible story. I sat there listening and shivered with excitement. But when he'd finished talking, Gustav simply laughed and said that this is what he'd heard in the cottages in his childhood. I'm sure we could hear stories like this in the village today too, even though they probably wouldn't share them with us. I'd gotten goose bumps hearing Gustav's story and wanted to know if anyone had ever found the tunnel. Oh no, he said, of course no one's

---

found it. Even though people claim this and that, everyone always knew it was nothing but a fairy tale. But I still wanted to know more. I wanted to know where that closed mine was located, what its name was. Gustav just shook his head. 'It's called Mervas,' he said, 'but I don't even think there's a road there anymore.'"

Kosti grew silent and Marta removed the cloth from her forehead. She lifted her head and looked at him.

"So was there a tunnel?" she asked quietly.

At first, Kosti didn't respond. He looked at her with an expression that was guarded but also begged understanding.

"Yes," he said at last. "There was a tunnel. There is a tunnel."

She lay down again with the cloth in her closed fist and looked at the bottom of the bed above her.

"It took me nearly a year to find the entrance to it," Kosti said in a low voice. "It's a tunnel through the mountain. It's been carved out by running water, of course. But it's enormous. It's beautiful. I walked in it for days and it just went on and on. It was like in a dream. And you know what, I found something down there. Something small. I'd like to show it to you, if you want to see it."

"That was one of the first things I thought when I first arrived here, in Mervas," Marta said, as if she hadn't heard him. "I didn't want to descend those stairs, didn't want to go down into the darkness where the water gleamed at the bottom. But as soon as I got here, I knew I had to do it. I had to."

"I understand," Kosti said.

"It's a fairy tale. Say it. Tell me it's a fairy tale. Tell me now."

"It is a fairy tale, Mart. Of course it's a fairy tale. It's our fairy tale. Yours and mine."

She inhaled.

"Then you can show me," she said. "Show me what you found down there."

Kosti rooted around in his pack for a while. Marta sat up. She followed his movements, the excitement he couldn't contain.

"Listen," he said to her, "why don't we go out on the steps for a little bit? Just for a while. We'll have more light out there."

They sat down next to each other at the top of the steps. He kept the object hidden in his hands.

"Here," he whispered, and let her see. "You see what it is?"

She did see. It was a Sámi silver brooch with small hanging charms around the edges. It was tarnished black, but completely intact.

"You see what it is?" he repeated.

Marta took the brooch carefully in her hand and examined it. She let her finger move over the protrusion in the middle and over the etched patterns.

"It's old," she said, without looking up.

"Yes, it's old," he agreed. "Of course it's old. And it's remained dry, it hasn't been in the water, it's remained dry down there in the tunnel ever since someone, whoever it could've been, dropped it. When I found it, I thought it was a greeting of sorts, that it was a message."

"From them?"

"Yes, sure, from them. But also a message about you. From you. That's what was so strange about it. That's what was so important. It was when I'd found this piece of jewelry that I turned around and started walking back. I knew I had to show it to you. I knew I couldn't keep going alone. I had to find the end of this story together with you. And I'll tell you something, although it was probably my imagination. I thought I smelled something in the air down there. Just as I'd bent down and was looking at the brooch, there was a breeze, a faint gust of air – it smelled of sun,

---

yes, it smelled of sun and daylight, as if the end of the tunnel was close, as if it was possible to get out, to get out of it – "

Marta put the brooch on her lap. She took Kosti's hand and raised it to her mouth to kiss it. She kissed the dry skin of his palm, kissed all the lines and grooves. She hid her face in his hand, filled it with the moisture of her breath. She wanted to keep her face there, enveloped by his hand, inside him, protected. And she felt his body leaning over hers, felt him crouch over her.

"I've prepared everything," he said gently. "All you have to do is trust me."

"You know what I'm thinking," she said, and looked up. "I'm thinking we're already there, standing at the opening to the island, blinded by all the light streaming over us."

"So you'll come with me?"

She took his hand in hers again, examined it and touched it. "Haven't you realized? I'll never let go of this hand again."

He grasped her face and stared at her, elated and eager again.

"You must promise me to be careful with your face, as careful with it as I would be. No more shards, promise me."

"No more shards."

He traced his finger lightly over her wounded cheek. "Good."

"Just tell me you've waited for me too."

"I've waited for you. You know that. I asked you to come."

"And I did," she said. "I came."